"Stop The Wedding. Now!" Cash Callahan Exclaimed.

There was dead silence in the church. You could have heard a snowflake fall. Cash pushed past the usher and headed down the aisle. At last the minister cleared his throat. "I don't think..." he began tentatively.

Cash didn't think, either, but that wasn't going to stop him. Maybe he'd got here a little later than he would have liked, but he'd come to prevent a disaster, and by God, he was going to prevent it.

He turned to face the assembled wedding guests "The guy who marries Milly Malone ought to be more than stable and dependable and reliable. He ought to love Milly more than any other man loves her. And *nobody* loves Milly the way I do." He paused and turned, and now he looked straight at her. "And Milly loves me, too." Another pause. "Don't you?"

Dear Reader,

Silhouette Desire is proud to launch three brand-new, emotional and romantic miniseries this month! We've got twin sisters switching places, sexy men who rise above their pasts and a ranching family marrying off their Texas daughters.

Along with our spectacular new miniseries, we're bringing you Anne McAllister's latest novel in her bestselling CODE OF THE WEST series, July's MAN OF THE MONTH selection, *The Cowboy Crashes a Wedding*. Next, a shy, no-frills librarian leads a fairy-tale life when she masquerades as her twin sister in Barbara McMahon's *Cinderella Twin*, book one of her IDENTICAL TWINS! duet. In *Seducing the Proper Miss Miller* by Anne Marie Winston, the town's black sheep and the minister's daughter cause a scandal with their sudden wedding.

Sexy Western author Peggy Moreland invites readers to get to know the McCloud sisters and the irresistible men who court them—don't miss the first TEXAS BRIDES book, *The Rancher's Spittin' Image*. And a millionaire bachelor discovers his secret heir in *The Tycoon's Son* by talented author Shawna Delacorte. A gorgeous loner is keeping quiet about *His Most Scandalous Secret* in the first book in Susan Crosby's THE LONE WOLVES miniseries.

So get to know the friends and families in Silhouette Desire's hottest new miniseries—and watch for more of their love stories in months to come!

Regards,

Melissa Senate

Melissa Senate
Senior Editor
Silhouette Books

Please address questions and book requests to:
Silhouette Reader Service
U.S.: 3010 Walden Ave., P.O. Box 1325, Buffalo, NY 14269
Canadian: P.O. Box 609, Fort Erie, Ont. L2A 5X3

ANNE McALLISTER
THE COWBOY CRASHES A WEDDING

SILHOUETTE *Desire*®

Published by Silhouette Books

America's Publisher of Contemporary Romance

SILHOUETTE BOOKS

ISBN 0-373-76153-8

THE COWBOY CRASHES A WEDDING

Books by Anne McAllister

Silhouette Desire

Cowboys Don't Cry #907
Cowboys Don't Quit #944
Cowboys Don't Stay #969
The Cowboy and the Kid #1009
Cowboy Pride #1034
The Cowboy Steals a Lady #1117
The Cowboy Crashes a Wedding #1153

Silhouette Special Edition

A Cowboy's Tears #1137

*Code of the West

ANNE McALLISTER

RITA Award-winning author Anne McAllister fell in love
with a cowboy when she was five years old. Tall, dark,
handsome lone-wolf types have appealed to her ever
since. "Me, for instance," her college professor husband
says. Well, yes. But even though she's been married to
the man of her dreams for over thirty years, she still likes
writing about those men of the West! And even though
she may take a break from cowboy heroes now and then,
she has lots more stories planned for the CODE OF THE
WEST. She is always happy to hear from readers, and if
you'd like, you can write to Anne at P.O. Box 3904,
Bozeman, Montana 59772. SASE appreciated.

For Pam,
who always helps me believe there's a
plot in there somewhere!

One

Cash could hear her laugh the moment he walked through the door.

He stood just inside the bar, unmoving, totally alert, like a wolf trying to catch a scent on the wind, listening for Milly's sound in the general uproar.

The Barrel was a noisy cowboy bar—people talked and laughed, the jukebox played, the TV blared—and the noise didn't stop at his arrival. In fact, no one even seemed to notice him at all.

Nor did he notice them as he listened. The cold winter wind slapped the door shut behind him. He stood still, listening.

And then he heard it again—gay, happy, musical. Milly. Laughing like she didn't have a care in the world.

He turned in the direction of the sound and spotted her then, sitting with three other women at a table near the window.

She had her back to him, but it didn't matter. He knew her back. He'd pressed his body against it on more than a few cold winters' nights. He knew the long dark hair that hung down it in a curtain almost to her waist. He'd twined his fingers through that hair, had buried his face in it, slept with his cheek against it. He even knew that shirt she was wearing. He'd torn the buttons off it once in his eagerness to love her.

Hell, he was still eager to love her.

And he'd have thought she'd be pretty eager to love him.

But she was marrying somebody else.

His brows drew down, and he moved, heading deliberately toward her table. He was maybe ten feet away when one of the girls looked up and saw him.

She stopped talking. Her smile faded. Her eyes widened. She went totally still. One by one the other girls did, too, until finally Milly turned to see what they were looking at.

For an instant her eyes widened just a little bit, too. But then they went blank and flat as stones as her gaze slid slowly up past Cash's gold Salinas winner's belt buckle to his rough, unshaven jaw and scowling face.

He shifted his weight slightly under her gaze. Okay, so maybe he didn't look like some Sir Galahad, but he hadn't taken the time to shave. He'd figured she would need him so much it wouldn't matter.

"Cash."

There was no welcome in her voice. No need, either. Her tone was as flat and disinterested as her eyes. She didn't look him in the eye.

Probably couldn't, Cash thought. She knew she was making a mistake. She just couldn't say so. Yet. She would. He knew she would.

"Milly." He said her name almost gently. Patiently. A hell of a lot more patiently than he felt. But he was willing to play along if this was the way she wanted it.

He didn't suppose it was really fair to Dutton, the guy she was engaged to at the moment, but that wasn't his problem. If she wanted to do things this way, that was fine by him.

He'd known what she was up to the minute her mother had told him where she was.

"The Barrel?" he'd said. "She went to The Barrel?" He'd started to smile. "Is she...tempting fate?"

Everyone knew the old story about how local women went to The Barrel right before their weddings.

"Just to be sure they've got the right man," Milly had told him once. One time, back during World War II sometime, one of them hadn't. She'd gone to The Barrel with her friends to celebrate her upcoming marriage—and had eloped with a sailor home on leave.

Since then a fair number of local women had gone to The Barrel to "tempt fate," as they called it.

Cash guessed Milly was doing the same thing. So, fine, he'd be happy to oblige her. He understood about a flair for the dramatic. He rode broncs, didn't he?

Now he waited. He tapped the toe of his boot.

"Go away, Cash," Milly said.

His brows drew down. "What do you mean, go away? I came all the way from Nebraska! Drove thirteen hours."

"Why? I didn't send you an invitation."

An invitation? To The Barrel? Of course not!

She meant to her wedding. And that was something else that galled him. They'd been lovers, hadn't they? Of course they had! For years! There wasn't anybody on earth closer to Milly Malone than he was.

And she hadn't even had the decency to invite him to see her get married!

Well, hell, it didn't matter, did it?

"I reckon I won't need one," he said as coolly as he could, "if there ain't going to be a wedding."

Milly's eyes bugged. No longer flat and disinterested like her voice, they raged with fury and sparkled with green fire. "There is most definitely going to be a wedding, Cash Callahan," she said through her teeth, and her voice wasn't flat and disinterested, either, now, "and you're not invited."

"Now that's what I call poor sportsmanship," Cash said, refusing to let her see that her words hurt. "I'd invite you if I was gettin' married."

"Fat chance! You'll never get married! You won't stay anywhere long enough. And who'd have you? A man whose idea of staying power is eight seconds max!"

That stung, too, but he wasn't admitting that, either.

"Aw, you know I can last longer than that, babe." He slanted her a wicked grin, designed to remind her of the times they'd spent in bed together when he'd lasted a whole lot longer than that. He remembered them well—and he knew she was remembering it, too.

She looked like there'd be fire coming out of her ears any second now.

Cash stepped back, wondering if maybe he'd overdone it a bit. He tugged on the brim of his hat. "You just think about that a little, sweetheart. Think about me."

"If I thought about you, I'd remember *all* the times we had," Milly said tartly. "The good ones and the bad ones—and mostly the ones where every time I turned around you were picking up to leave me again."

"Now, darlin'—"

"But I'm not going to think about you, Cash. You're done. Finished. Over. Past." She lifted her glass to her lips and drained it, then set it down with a thump and looked straight into Cash's eyes. "Gone," she said. "Like that."

He blinked. His brows lifted, then lowered. He scratched the back of his neck. He looked hopefully at the other three girls. Two looked away. Only one, Milly's friend, Poppy, whom she worked for, looked back. She looked disgusted.

About the same way he felt. "You talk some sense into her," he said to Poppy.

"This is not my problem."

"Well, she won't listen to me."

"Maybe you're not saying the right words."

"Huh?"

"Forget it, Poppy," Milly said sharply. She poured herself another glass from the pitcher on the table then lifted her glass in toast. "Here's to the future. To love and marriage. To happily ever after. To me...and Mike."

All three of her friends raised their glasses and clinked them against Milly's.

Then quite deliberately Milly turned away and started talking about the flowers she and Poppy were doing for the wedding.

Cash stood there, staring down at her. But she didn't look at him again. She didn't even acknowledge his presence. It was as if he had vanished into thin air.

"Prettiest things you ever did see," she said just as if he wasn't breathing down her neck. "Long-stemmed yellow roses and—"

Cash let out a long, disgusted breath. Then he stepped around so that he could look down into Milly's stubborn face, and he jerked his head toward the bar. "You talk about those flowers long as you want. You talk about weddin' cakes and petits fours and all that claptrap. I'll wait. I'll be right over there when you need me. But I'm not waitin' forever, Milly. So you just give a shout, darlin', when you want to start makin' sense."

Sense?

When *she* wanted to make sense!?

Well, that was Cash Callahan for you—arrogant and wrong headed to the end.

How dare he come barging in here, big as life and twice as sassy, and act like she ought to fall into his mouth like a ripe plum?

She'd been the ripe plum in Cash Callahan's life far too long—and look what it had got her: nothing.

He wasn't any closer to marrying her now than he'd been when they'd met five years ago! And if he thought for one minute she was going to change her mind and give up a great guy like Mike Dutton and a chance at marital happiness just so she could be available whenever he deigned to pass through town for the rest of her life, well...

"He can sit there and rot for all I care," she said in a tone quite loud enough to carry to the bar where Cash had settled in and was already pouring himself a second glass of whiskey. "And how dare he tell me *he* wouldn't wait forever! How long does he think I waited, for heaven's sake?"

"He doesn't think, Milly," her friend Bev, the librarian, pointed out calmly. "That's the trouble with Cash."

"He always just expected you to be there," her other friend Tina said.

It was nothing that Milly didn't already know. "I don't want to talk about Cash," she said firmly. "I want to celebrate my marriage. I want to laugh, to sing, to dance—"

"Here?" Both Bev and Tina looked at her, askance.

"In my heart," Milly said. "I need to laugh and sing and dance in my heart."

Poppy reached over and squeezed her hand. "Go for it," she said. "Go for what you want." Poppy's eyes were wide and sincere as she picked up her glass and toasted Milly.

Taking courage, Milly drank another glass. She tried not to look at Cash. She didn't need to in order to know he was there. If Cash was anywhere within a hundred miles, her internal radar could sense him. She'd been attuned to Cash Callahan since the night she'd met him.

Well, damn it, it was time to get retuned.

Five years was long enough to be a fool. She was done with Cash. Finished. Through.

She raised the glass of ginger ale she was drinking, then looked over at Cash and lifted her glass in a mock toast.

He didn't pretend not to notice her.

"To me," she mouthed. "And Mike."

Cash glared at her over the top of a whiskey bottle, his eyes accusing her all the while.

He debated sending over a pitcher of beer with his compliments. He went so far as to ask the waitress what they were drinking, and smiled to himself when he found out it was ginger ale.

"Two of them had a beer apiece," the girl told him. "But they aren't real heavy drinkers."

At least that much of Milly hadn't changed.

Her head sure had. He couldn't imagine what she was thinking—hadn't been able to for a good long time now. He tried to figure it out, but every time he got close, his glass was empty and he needed a bit more to get further on with the puzzle, and then somehow he had to start over.

He wasn't sure how many whiskeys he'd had when a man slid onto the bar stool next to his.

"Long time, no see, Callahan."

Cash looked up to see fellow roughstock rider, Shane Nichols, settle in.

"Hey." Cash gave him a nod and as much of a grin as he could muster under the circumstances.

Shane Nichols was the Montana equivalent of a good ole boy. A little impetuous now and then. A little crazy sometimes—he was a bull rider, after all—but a better man didn't exist. And he'd commiserate. He knew about a guy's priorities. Cash pushed the bottle in his direction.

Shane looked longingly at it, but shook his head, then asked the bartender for a ginger ale.

"Ginger ale?" Cash looked at him, disbelieving.

"Doc's orders." Shane lifted his hand and waggled it at Cash. It was wrapped in a cast—and then Cash remembered. Shane had lost his thumb in a freak accident a while back—something to do with a trailer and a runaway horse—and had managed to have it sewn back on.

"Doc don't want your thumb to get drunk?" Cash asked with a faint grin.

"Somethin' like that," Shane agreed. "Whole list of things it can't do. Whole list of things *I* can't do." He looked glum. He tipped up the glass and downed it all in one gulp, fidgeted on the stool, then ordered another.

"Like ridin'," Cash guessed. He sat in commiserating silence for a moment, then said, "I drew Deliverance down in Houston."

Shane grinned. "Oughta win big on that 'un."

"Hope to. Gotta stay on 'im first."

"No sweat. Ridden him before, haven't you?"

Cash nodded. "Twice."

"No sweat then."

"Bucked off 'im twice, though, too," Cash admitted.

"Aw, well, that don't count," Shane said. "Gotta look on the bright side." He looked down at his casted hand and sighed.

Cash, having already looked on the bright side, sighed, too. His gaze strayed to the women by the window once more. Shane's gaze followed. An interested look flickered across his face. He half stood.

Cash saw the look and grimaced. "Don't bother," he said bitterly. "She's taken."

Shane's gaze swiveled to meet his. "Huh?"

Cash scowled into his glass. "Don't see why she couldn'ta waited," he muttered.

Shane settled back onto the bar stool. "Huh? She who? Waited for what?"

"Milly." Cash jerked his head toward the women again.

Shane followed his gaze curiously. Cash could see him sizing them up as they laughed and talked. "Who's Milly?"

"My girlfriend. *Ex*-girlfriend." Cash poured himself another whiskey. He tipped the glass and downed the whiskey in a gulp, then smacked the glass back down on the counter again. "Damn her."

Shane eased around to study the women at length. His eyes got wider the longer he looked. Cash wasn't surprised. They didn't fit into the bar scene. Cash knew that.

Shane had been to enough bars that he knew it, too. "What're they doing here?"

"Celebratin'," Cash muttered into his glass.

Shane lifted a quizzical brow.

"It's a tradition," Cash explained grudgingly. "Local girls do it. Come to The Barrel with their girlfriends just before they get married."

"How come?"

Cash shrugged, annoyed. "How the hell should I know? Damn fool notion if you ask me. Milly says it started when some ol' gal dared another one to check out the rest of the men before she tied the knot. Temptin' fate, she calls it."

Shane raised a quizzical brow.

Cash poured himself another shot, thumped the bottle down again, gulped the whiskey and answered the unspoken question. "Not likely." Then he scowled once more in the direction of the table of women.

Shane nursed his ginger ale and studied them, too. "Interesting notion," he said at last. "Never heard of such a thing in Elmer. Of course, we only have the Dew Drop up there. Not that many fellas worth lookin' at.''

"Only takes one.''

None of the women looked at them. Cash's fingers tightened on his glass.

"Which one's Milly?'' Shane asked at last.

"The pretty one.'' Cash didn't take his eyes off the glass in front of him. "Long dark hair. Green eyes.''

"Ah.'' There was a smile in Shane's voice. Cash could hear it. "Yeah,'' Shane said, properly appreciative, "she's somethin', all right.''

"She's that,'' Cash agreed grimly.

"How come she's your ex, then?''

"'Cause she got tired of waiting.'' Cash swirled the whiskey in his glass, then took a swallow and shut his eyes. "Just like a woman. I'da waited for her. I'da waited till the cows came home for her! But no, she didn't want to wait. Said life was passin' her by, said all her friends were gettin' married, when were we gettin' married? Hell, do I look like I'm ready to get married?'' He glared defiantly at Shane.

Obediently Shane shook his head. "Nope. Sure don't.''

Cash gave a quick nod, glad at least that Shane understood. "Eventu'ly, I told her. We'll do it eventu'ly. Gimme time, I said. Hell, I wasn't askin' for forever! Then last summer a friend of hers was gettin' married and they came here for their damned ol' girls' night out before the wedding, and she met *him*.''

"Him?''

"Dutton. Mike Dutton. God's gift to women...or at least to Milly Malone. She's marryin' him Saturday.''

"Whoa.'' Shane's eyes got wide.

"That's what I said,'' Cash growled. "Didn't do me a damn bit of good.'' He finished his whiskey and glowered in the direction of the women at the table. "She tol' me to take a hike. Tol' me I'd lost out. Lost her.'' His fists clenched and he started to stand, but the whiskey was stronger than he was, and he wavered, then dropped back on the bar stool again. "Hell," he muttered. "'S hell."

"I reckon," Shane said sympathetically.

"It is," Cash affirmed. His mind felt fuzzy and out of kilter. Like his life. "Don't make a bit a sense. She doesn't love him! She loves *me!*"

"Course she does," Shane agreed, his voice soothing.

But Cash wasn't in the mood to be soothed. He was in the mood to be miserable, and he was more than halfway there.

"She'll be sorry." He set his elbows on the bar and propped his head up with his fists. "She'll be damn sorry. She'll wake up Sund'y mornin' married to the jerk an' realize she made a mistake. But then it'll be too late." His eyes shut, something stung in behind the lids. His throat felt tight, thick. It ached. "'S already too late," he said, his words slurring. And as the truth of his words hit home, he put his head down on the bar.

"It's never too late," Shane said flatly. "She's not married yet. Talk to her. Tell her—"

"She won't listen." Cash wiggled his brows and managed to get his eyes open again. "Tried."

"Make her listen. Insist."

"Yeah, right." Cash sighed. But Shane was right. He was always right. A man could do worse than listen to Shane. "I'd stop the weddin' if I was gonna be here," he said wistfully. "She'd have to listen then."

Shane flashed a grin. "Reckon so." He turned his head and shot a quick glance in the direction of the laughing women.

Cash saw Poppy look back at his buddy, then she turned her gaze on him.

Once upon a time Cash thought he could have counted

on Poppy to make Milly see sense. She was a good 'un, that Poppy. Leastways he'd always thought so.

But Poppy seemed to be taking Dutton's side. What was it she'd said? Somethin' about Cash sayin' the wrong words?

Hell, he'd be tickled to say the right ones if she'd like to tell him what they were! But all she did was give him a longer, almost pitying look, then deliberately turned back to Milly.

Shane frowned, then picked up his ginger ale and looked at Cash. "Why don't you?"

"Can't. Told you. Drew me a great bronc down in Houston. Deliverance." He said the horse's name reverently. "So I can't stay." He shrugged. "If she'd wait, I could be back on Tuesday…"

But she wouldn't wait. Cash knew that.

She'd go right ahead and marry ol' Dutton just because Cash wouldn't be there to stop her.

Both men glared at the table of women. Then Shane shook his head, disgusted. "Women," he muttered.

"'Bout ready to hit the road?" Dennis Cooper, one of Cash's traveling partners, clapped a hand on Cash's shoulder. He'd come in shortly after Cash had settled at the bar. He'd been ready to leave then, but Cash couldn't. He'd told Milly he would stay. He'd said he would wait until she came to her senses.

Now, more hours and more whiskey later than he wanted to think about, she'd done nothing of the kind. She was just about out of time.

Wordlessly Cash stared at the almost empty bottle, then at the woman whose stubbornness had made him drain it.

Denny glanced at his watch. "We better be makin' tracks if we're gonna get out ahead of the storm."

Cash frowned. "What storm?"

"Mark's been listenin' to the radio. Says there's a big

one comin'. Blowin' in by morning, they say. So I say it's about time we headed south.''

Cash considered that. He considered Milly.

She lifted her glass and toasted him with it. "To me." He saw her form the words. "To Mike."

Cash poured the last of the whiskey into his glass and swirled the liquid, staring into it. Then, "Guess so," he said. "Ain't nothin' left for me here."

He shut his eyes, tipped his head back and drained the glass. It didn't burn near as bad as the first glass had. Maybe he was getting anesthetized. He opened his eyes, blinked rapidly and shoved himself to his feet. "Let's go."

He gave Shane a soft jab to the upper arm. "Take it easy. Don't do anything I wouldn't do."

Shane grinned. "Leavin' the field wide open, aren'tcha?"

Cash managed a harsh laugh. "Damn straight."

Then he tugged his hat down tight on his head and squared his shoulders. Bow-legged, swivel-hipped, he followed Denny toward the door.

He wasn't going to look at Milly. But he couldn't help it.

He had to look, had to give her one last chance. So as he passed, he turned his head. It was no furtive glance, no quick look. He didn't even blink.

But Milly didn't even glance his way. She just lifted her glass and clinked it against Poppy's, and together they laughed at some toast Poppy was making.

Cash's jaw tightened. His fists clenched. He kept on walking. But he could still hear them. He heard them laugh again as he reached the door.

He put his hand on it, paused. Waited. *Stop me, Milly. Stop me.*

But she didn't.

She didn't even seem to notice when, shoulders hunched, head bent, Cash pushed his way out the door.

He left.

She finished her ginger ale. She thanked her friends for coming with her. "Now it's official," she assured them gaily. "I'm marrying Mike. No one at The Barrel swept me off my feet."

"Only because he could barely stand on them," Poppy said in a dry tone as they gathered their coats to leave.

"What are you talking about?" Milly said, keeping a smile pasted on her face. She tugged on her coat and began fumbling with the buttons.

"You know what I'm talking about. You know *who* I'm talking about."

Well, yes. But she debated lying about it. Poppy would know she was lying, though. Poppy knew about those sorts of things.

"I don't know why he came," Milly mumbled at last.

"Because he's in love with you." The answer was quick and unequivocal, as matter-of-fact as Poppy always was.

"He doesn't know what love is."

"Not grown-up love, I'll grant you that," Poppy said. "Here, let me button that. You'd think you were the one drinking the beer not the ginger ale." With deft fingers and complete concentration, she buttoned Milly's coat for her. "But he cares. He's just hopeless at saying so."

"It's too late for him to say so," Milly said firmly. "I'm marrying Mike."

They walked out into the cold winter night and Milly felt a shiver run through her. She'd been shivering a lot lately. Feeling cold a lot. Wishing for warm arms around her, desperate for a warm body to hold her.

Mike's.

She wanted Mike.

"I'm surprised he showed up," Poppy went on after they said good-night to Bev and Tina and headed toward their cars.

Cash, she was talking about. Still. Always Cash. Milly didn't want to think about Cash.

"I'm marrying Mike," she said firmly.

"If that's what you want," Poppy said mildly.

"It's what I want! I don't want Cash!" Milly knew she was raising her voice. She knew she was making a fuss. She knew Poppy didn't believe a word she said. "I don't want Cash," she said plaintively again in a voice that was barely more than a whisper. "I don't!"

Poppy took Milly's hands in hers and rubbed them briskly. "I know," she soothed. "It'll be all right. It's just nerves."

"And Cash," Milly said wryly, unable to help it, bringing up his name herself.

"And Cash," Poppy agreed with a grin.

"I'll feel better when it's over," Milly said firmly.

"Of course you will."

"It's just the wait."

"Yes."

"We should have eloped."

"No," Poppy said at once. "You're doing it right. You wanted to do it in front of God and everyone. You said so. To show your commitment. To make a statement."

"Yes," Milly agreed. But it seemed like the statement was taking way too much out of her. She wanted it over— all of it: the waiting, the wedding, the promises. She wanted to be safely committed to Michael George Dutton, for ever and ever. Amen.

Poppy gave her hands a squeeze and then smiled an encouraging smile. "You made it. You got through tonight. Cash is gone. Stop worrying. The worst is over."

"Yes." It was. Of course it was. She'd seen him for the

last time. He'd come. He'd seen. He hadn't conquered. Milly pasted on the bravest smile she could muster. "Yes," she said again. "It's over."

Later that night when she was lying alone in her bedroom she told herself that again. "It's over."

Sometimes, though, she thought that the love she and Cash Callahan had shared wasn't so much over as it was love that had never really begun. Not mutual love, anyway.

She'd loved.

Cash had...passed through.

Mike was a man for the long haul. He would be there through thick and thin. He had held her hand and kissed away her tears more often than she cared to remember.

Well, she swore to herself now, he wouldn't have to kiss away any more of her tears. She was done crying.

She was done with Cash. She was marrying Mike on Saturday. It was, she assured herself, the first day of the rest of her life.

She wondered why that didn't cheer her up.

TWO

Denny was asleep in the passenger seat. Walt and Mark were sprawled out in the back. They'd stopped to pick up a rookie bronc rider just outside Cheyenne, and even the rookie—after what seemed like a thousand hours of eager bouncing off the walls of the van and a million and a half meaningless questions about how much farther it was to Houston and didn't they think ol' Hammerhead was a terrific draw, and how much did they reckon he'd win—had settled into a restless slumber.

Cash drove on.

He'd tried to sleep when they left Livingston. Denny had driven then. But Cash's mind was too busy replaying the sight of Milly laughing and smiling with her friends, then looking cold and unblinking at him. He couldn't sleep. He'd stared out the window, drummed his fingers on his knee, chewed his lower lip, tugged again and again at the brim of his hat. If he'd taken it off in the bar, he'd have wondered if he'd accidentally grabbed someone else's. His felt too damn tight.

"Sit still, for cryin' out loud," Denny said more than once. And finally he'd said, "I'll pull over if you've gotta pee."

"'M fine," Cash muttered.

But he wasn't fine. He wasn't fine at all.

He thought it would get better by the time it got light. But by the time it was light, it wasn't better. He thought it would get better by the time they got to Colorado Springs. But by the time they got to Colorado Springs, nothing had changed. He thought maybe he was rushing things, that maybe the Texas border would do the trick.

But they'd be in Texas in less than half an hour now, and things weren't looking up.

He missed Milly.

He wanted Milly.

He couldn't imagine a future without Milly.

But sure as shootin', if she married Mike that was the way the future was going to be.

There was no way he'd be stopping to see her every time he traveled through Livingston anymore. There was no way he'd call her on the phone at two in the morning just to say hi and see what she was doing.

"What'm I doing? I'm sleepin', Cash," she always said in that grumbly sleepy little voice he loved. That was *why* he called her up then. Didn't she know that?

Probably she did.

That's probably why the last time he'd called, she'd said flatly, "Talking to Mike," and she'd sounded very matter-of-fact and not sleepy at all.

Cash had almost slammed the phone down in his disgust. *Talking to Mike?* At two o'clock in the morning?

"Well, tell him to go home. He's there too damned late," he'd said in his own grumbly voice.

But Milly didn't say, "I know." She'd just said, "Good-bye, Cash," and then, damned if she hadn't hung up on him!

No, if she married Mike on Saturday, Cash wouldn't be calling her again. Ever.

She'd have to call him—to tell him what a mistake she'd made.

But somehow, deep down in his gut, he knew she never would.

Damn it. He pinched the bridge of his nose and rubbed a hand across his forehead. The sign flashed past, welcoming them to Texas.

It looked big and wide and lonely as hell.

Exactly the way he felt.

"I'm goin' back."

Denny jerked in the seat next to him. "Wha'?" He squinted groggily at Cash.

"I'm goin' back." He said it again. Firmer. Louder. As much to convince himself as Denny. And the words sounded better this time, more positive. Right. "'M goin' back."

The third time Cash said it, Walt raised his head, too. "We forget somethin'?" he mumbled.

"No. I'm goin' back to Livingston."

Both Dennis and Walt sat up straight then. "The hell are you talkin' about?" Dennis demanded. "We're practically in Houston. We're goin' to Houston!"

"We gotta go to Houston. *You* gotta go to Houston!" Walt said. "You're riding Deliverance."

"No," Cash said. "I ain't."

When he said it, he almost expected the world to end, the cymbals to crash, the curtain to come whooshing down. He'd lived for rodeo his entire life—since he'd been no higher than his daddy's gold belt buckle—and had aimed to get him one, too.

Now he had a couple dozen. Oh, not *the* buckle, the one he'd always been after. He'd been to the National Finals Rodeo five times—but he'd never brought home the gold.

He was pretty sure now he never was going to bring home the gold. But he'd been going after it so long, he didn't know what else to do with himself.

It was what he did...in between visits to Milly.

And that, when he thought about it, was the unvarnished honest-to-God truth.

In the last couple of years or so—he wasn't exactly sure how long; Cash wasn't big on abstract analysis—it wasn't the rodeos that he'd measured time by, it was when he was next going to see Milly.

He'd been sort of gearing up to ask her... Well, maybe not exactly to ask her; he still shied away from the *M* word like a mustang from a hackamore. But if he hadn't exactly been ready to ask her yet, he was willing to hint that sometime he might be willing to make their arrangement a little more permanent.

And then what had she done?

She'd changed the locks on the doors!

She'd started dating another man!

She'd gone and got herself engaged to the jerk!

And now she was going to marry him!

Unless Cash stopped her.

They'd shared too much. Five years. Five unbelievable years. Christ, they'd been kids when they'd met that first time...when she'd jeered and he'd scowled, when she'd smiled and he'd winked...and—

God, he *had* to stop her!

He hadn't been going to stop at Wilsall for the rodeo.

It wasn't a big rodeo, didn't pay all that much. There were dozens of other rodeos he could have gone to that summer Saturday five years ago.

But they weren't going to be that far from Wilsall, he and his buddies—and one of them, Pete, had grown up nearby, so it made sense to stop, get a home-cooked meal, do a little laundry and hit the road again.

"We could make more in Greeley," Rod argued.

But Cash had sided with Pete. He was just as happy not to have to spend long hours in a car, anyway. He'd cracked his ribs in Ponca, Nebraska, two weeks before. He'd strained his shoulder in Window Rock. He still had stitches in his jaw from a flying hoof he'd come in contact with in Prescott. At least he thought it was in Prescott. He'd been so damn many places he couldn't quite remember where he'd done what anymore.

But last night in Butte, he'd pulled the shoulder again. It hurt like sin, and he wasn't even sure if he should ride. Actually he was damned sure he shouldn't ride, but he wasn't letting that stop him. He needed the money. He had barely enough to buy gas, let alone food.

He was going to ride in Wilsall. *And* have one of Pete's mother's home-cooked meals. *And* do his laundry, if she'd let him. *And* maybe—just maybe—sleep in a bed for a change instead of on a pile of saddle blankets in the back of Rod's truck.

At least that was the plan.

Some of it worked. The laundry, for instance. Pete's mother, apparently having been deprived of opportunities for maternal doting for a long time, actually volunteered to do laundry for all of them while they caught forty winks. Pete, of course, because it was his home, got his bed. Rod took the other one while Cash was still bringing his laundry bag in from the truck.

"I'm afraid you'll have to make do with the sofa." Pete's mother apologized to him.

Cash didn't care. The sofa was a heck of a lot more

comfortable than the saddle blankets. Smelled better, too, he decided once he'd had a shower.

He felt a damn sight better, too, once he got outside Pete's mother's home-cooked meal. It was the best steak he could ever remember. He couldn't even recall the last time he'd put his belly around that big a meal. It almost hurt to move when he got up from the table. In fact, it did hurt, but that was owing more to his cracked ribs and strained shoulder than to Mrs. Reed's cooking.

"Sure do want to thank you, ma'am," he said to her as he carried his dishes to the sink.

"My pleasure," she assured him. "You stop by anytime."

"Yes, ma'am." Cash nodded in agreement, but he knew he wouldn't. He barely ever traveled the same roads twice. Not often, anyway. It just wasn't a part of his life-style.

"It isn't civilized, the way you boys live," his own mother had said more than once.

Cash agreed, but he didn't really care. It was fun, it was occasionally lucrative, and since he'd turned twenty-one three years ago, it was pretty much legal. Besides, he'd never put much stock in the value of civilization.

Still, he felt more civilized than he usually did when they finally got to the rodeo that evening. He thought he probably looked almost civilized, too, dressed in his spanking clean Wranglers and his fresh-pressed bright red shirt. The girls he passed on the way back behind the chutes seemed pretty impressed, though he figured it was probably more on account of the contestant's number the rodeo secretary had slapped on his back than because he was a prime example of American manhood on the hoof.

Whatever reason they were looking at him for, though, Cash didn't mind!

He gave them a smile to go with his swagger, and those

who batted their lashes at him got an even wider smile and a conspiratorial wink to go with it.

He and Rod and Pete wouldn't be leaving town until tomorrow morning. He'd spend the night on Pete's mother's sofa bed if he had to—and be glad for it—but a fellow ought to try to better himself if he could.

That's what his daddy had always said, and about this, at least, Cash believed him.

Cash was all for short-term goals. A nice soft wide bed and a pretty lady to go with it sounded like a damn fine goal for this evening.

First, though, there was the little matter of a bronc to be ridden—eight seconds on a roan gelding called Roscoe's Revenge. Cash had never heard of Roscoe's Revenge. Wilsall wasn't a big rodeo. Roscoe's Revenge wasn't even a very big horse. How hard could it be? he thought, when he settled himself over the horse's back and wrapped the rein around his hand.

Harder than it looked.

Harder than he thought.

But not as hard as the ground he landed on a full two seconds shy of the necessary eight.

Damn, his ribs hurt! Damn, his shoulder hurt! Damn, his butt hurt!

And scrambling to his feet amid the smattering of "hard-luck cowboy" applause didn't do a lot for his pride, either.

Cash slapped his hat angrily against his leg as he hobbled toward the fence. "Give 'im a little more," the announcer urged the crowd. "You know it's all the poor boy's gonna take home with him tonight."

"Damn it to hell," Cash muttered as he flung himself over the fence rail.

There was a sudden audible inhalation of breath, and his gaze jerked up. He found himself staring into wide, astonished green eyes—big, beautiful female eyes—the most beautiful eyes he'd ever seen. They belonged to a girl sitting in the front row right next to the chutes.

"He fwore," a childish voice piped loudly and cheerfully. "I thought you said cowboys don't fwear?"

Cash dragged his gaze away from the gorgeous eyes to see the small boy sitting next to her.

"Real cowboys don't," the girl said primly.

Cash turned his gaze back to her, scowling and revising his opinion of her eyes as he did so. They weren't all that special.

But they didn't flinch, either. They just looked right at him, hopefully, expectantly...and waited.

Waited? For what?

"Or at least they apologize," she said at last.

Cash's scowl deepened. He knew a challenge when he heard one. Well, he wasn't going to do it. He had no use for prissy women. But she didn't look prissy, or particularly judgmental, come to that. The look she gave him was almost hopeful, as if she was counting on him.

Hell. Cash revised that. Heck.

Damn—darn it. He didn't want to offend little children! But he'd had a good ride going! Two more lousy seconds and he'd have had gas money for the rest of the month.

The little boy stuck his thumb in his mouth and regarded Cash solemnly.

Cash gave a quick jerk of his head and muttered, "Sorry." It was the least he could say, so he said it.

The smile he got paid him back tenfold. Cripes, it damned near blinded him! He stumbled back and almost fell off the blasted fence.

"Whoa! 'Sa matter? He kick ya in the head?" Rod demanded. He reached over from the rail beside the chute and hauled Cash the rest of the way over the fence. "You all right?"

"Fine," Cash muttered. But he wasn't.

He'd never had a reaction like that to any woman in his life! It was like the one time he'd been fool enough to ride a bull and got his head butted for his trouble. He felt dazed. Reeling.

It couldn't just be from a smile. Could it?

Naw. Of course not. He must've hit his head, too.

But as Rod hauled him away, Cash twisted his head to take another look, willing the girl to look at him, to smile again.

But the next rider had just burst from the gate and the little boy yelled, "Lookit!" and the girl's attention was lost.

"C'mon. I'm up. Pull my rope," Rod said to him.

"Rope?"

"Rope," Rod repeated as if he were teaching Cash a foreign language. "Geez. Maybe you oughta get your head X-rayed."

"Maybe." Cash shook his head, stumbled over the rail and helped Rod pull his rope. Then he had to help Pete with his. Then one of the steer wrestlers asked him to haze.

When he finally had time to glance that way again, the girl—whoever she was—was gone.

"Only half an hour," Rod promised, his footsteps quickening as they headed toward the hall where the dance music was already blaring.

"Half an hour?" Cash balked. He was tired and irritable and out of sorts. He'd won no money, his new red shirt had a rip in it, and everything he owned seemed to hurt. He damned well didn't want to spend half an hour propping up a wall while Rod put the make on one of Wilsall's willing women.

Rod had placed third. He had money in his wallet, a smile on his face and no aches and pains to speak of. Luck was on his side. He'd probably even find a lovely lady to spend the night with.

Cash, for the moment a realist, knew he wouldn't. He wanted to lie down. Anywhere. And he didn't even care if it was alone. Mrs. Reed's couch sounded damned good right now.

"Fifteen minutes," Rod said. "If I haven't met a girl in fifteen minutes we'll go."

Cash scowled. "Five," he bargained. "Shouldn't take you more than that."

Rod flashed him a grin. "You got more faith in me than I do. Ten, then. Reckon I can charm one in ten. Get yourself a beer and stand by the door. If I don't come in ten minutes, catch a ride with somebody and leave me the truck, okay?"

Cash grunted. But that was fair. There had been times he'd made Rod wait for him. He got a beer and parked himself against the wall to watch. He was a pretty fair dancer when all his body parts were in working order. Tonight he could count the ones that worked on the fingers of one hand.

He probably should have put an elastic bandage back around his ribs after Rod had cut off the tape after Cash's ride. But he'd got busy, and then he'd decided to do it when they got back to Pete's place. That might've been a mistake.

His ribs hurt, and they made him feel a little vulnerable in a crowd like this. One good elbow and—the very thought made him wince.

The hard beat of the honky-tonk tune blaring over the speakers found a rhythm in the pulse of his breath against his ribs. He tried to breathe more shallowly. His gaze found Rod, chatting with a cute little blonde next to the soft-drink table. Rod grinned an "aw shucks" grin and Cash watched cynically as the girl dimpled in response. Then Rod scratched the back of his head and shuffled his feet. The girl batted her lashes and simpered.

Cash glanced at his watch. Seven minutes and counting. Yeah, Rod would probably make it. Cash saw him cock his head and hold out a hand to the girl. She smiled and put hers in his. Rod swept her into the dance.

Cash shut his eyes and shook his head.

When he opened them again, the music had stopped. Rod and the girl were nowhere to be seen. Couples milled and mingled. Another tune, louder and brassier than the first, began.

Cash took a swallow of his beer, wishing for something stronger. Not just to dull the pain. It wasn't just the pain. God knew he hurt. But it was more than that.

For all his buoyancy earlier in the evening, he'd been whistling in the dark and he knew it. He hadn't been making the rides lately. He hadn't seen the pay window in damn near three weeks. Sure, a guy had bad luck now and then. Cash understood that and could be philosophical if he had to be.

But being full was good, too. Meals like the one Pete's mother had made for them this afternoon were getting fewer and farther between. Philosophy was all well and good, but it only kept your belly from aching for just so long. He had to start winning.

He caught sight of Rod again, grinning like the Cheshire cat now, tipping back and forth on the soles of his boots and damn near drooling over the girl he was trying to impress. "Get on with it," Cash muttered. He glanced at his watch impatiently. Four and a half minutes to go.

He took another pull on his beer and shifted his weight from one boot to the other, wincing as he did so.

"Did you hurt yourself?"

For a second he didn't think the soft feminine voice was directed at him. He barely heard it anyway above the music, talk and laughter. But when the words were repeated, he glanced around—and saw her.

She stood just three feet away and was looking right at him, big beautiful green eyes full of concern—the girl from the rodeo.

"Er," Cash said, jerking up straight. His first impulse was to say no, he hadn't hurt himself. He was tough. Of course he was. Cowboys were. It was a rule of the road.

But women didn't always want a guy to be tough, did they? Sometimes they liked to fuss over a fellow, sympathize with him. Maybe rub his back. Kiss him and make it better.

How maudlin was that? Pretty, Cash had to admit. But he couldn't help the grimace as he turned. He reached back and rubbed the nape of his neck. "Just a little stiff," he allowed. Then he did his own version of the "aw, shucks" grin. "I've been hurt lots worse."

"You have?" The jade eyes got even bigger. She looked really worried now.

Cash swallowed carefully. "Yes, ma'am. Busted my leg in Window Rock last year. Got thirty-eight stitches in my ear from a bull in Pendleton soon as I came back. These—" he touched the line of the most recent ones he'd got only last Sunday "—ain't nothin' compared to that. It's my shoulder hurts the most tonight," he confided. "An' my ribs. Cracked a couple of 'em a while back."

She didn't say a word, just stared.

Cash wondered if he'd overplayed his hand. Most women were cooing and clucking and patting at him by this point in his recitation. This girl looked like she was afraid to touch him.

He cleared his throat and offered his hand. "My name's Cash Callahan."

"I know."

He blinked. "You do?"

She reddened slightly. "I looked up your number on the program."

"Oh." He felt his cheeks warm, too. "Er, yeah." Of course she had! Lots of girls did. He knew that. Why wasn't he thinking? Why was he staring at her like he was some junior high kid who'd never talked to a girl?

She still hadn't taken his hand. He reached out and took a gentle hold of her shoulder and turned her around.

She looked over her shoulder at him, a questioning expression on her face. He shrugged. "You're not wearin' a number. And I don't have a program."

The color in her cheeks deepened. "I'm Milly Malone." She turned back and took his hand, shook it for barely more than an instant, then dropped it and knotted her fingers together, looking down at them.

Cash was charmed. "Milly Malone," he repeated. He didn't know why, but it made him smile. She made him smile. His gaze narrowed just a little. "How come you don't think I'm a real cowboy, Milly Malone?"

She looked up quickly. "I shouldn't have said that."

A corner of Cash's mouth lifted. "Reckon you were right—about the swearin' part. I shouldn't've said it. Not in front of a kid. I was just...steamed." He shook his head in frustration. "I should've ridden him."

"He was mean."

Cash blinked. Broncs weren't mean. Not most of 'em. Certainly not this one. But if she wanted to think so... He scratched his jaw. "Maybe just a little," he allowed.

"He almost stepped on you."

"Yeah." Then honesty compelled him to add, "But he wasn't tryin' to. Now bulls, that's different. They try to do you in."

Milly Malone gave a small shudder. "I didn't want to watch the bulls."

"Most people, it's what they like. They're hopin' for a crash."

She shuddered. "Not me. It gives me the creeps."

"Guys who ride 'em know what they're doin'," Cash assured her. "They understand the risks."

But Milly Malone just shook her head. "I'm glad you don't ride bulls," she said and once more looked up at him with those glorious green eyes of hers.

Cash had to suck in his breath. "Never," he said stoutly. Then honesty reared its ugly head again, and he found himself backing off that, too. "Well, I have," he admitted. "A couple of times. Well, maybe twenty or so. But not too often. Don't like 'em as much as I like broncs. But I do like to eat."

Milly's eyes widened. "Eat?"

A wry grin touched his mouth. "Sometimes I need to do both to make enough money to keep goin'."

"You could quit and get a real job."

Now it was Cash's eyes widening. In horror. "God, no," he said fervently.

And suddenly Milly laughed.

It was a full-throated, marvelous sound. As if he'd actually said something funny instead of the absolute truth. But it didn't matter. He loved her laugh as much as he'd loved her smile. It made her whole face light up. It made her green eyes sparkle.

"I like what I do," he told her. "And I get by. At the moment I've got enough to feed me—and you, too," he added, stretching the truth just a bit. "How 'bout gettin' something to eat?"

Milly hesitated. "How about a soft drink?"

He wasn't sure if she wasn't hungry or if she somehow guessed how badly straitened his finances actually were. Whichever, he didn't care. He just wanted some more time with her, some more smiles from her.

And maybe...

Maybe he wouldn't have to spend the night on Mrs. Reed's sofa after all.

Milly had never been to a rodeo in her life.

She'd never picked up a man in her life.

She'd certainly never invited one back to her apartment before!

But then, until last week she'd never had an apartment of her own. It just went to show what a wild woman she'd been hiding deep inside her all of her nineteen years!

Her mother had been right to worry when Milly had come home after her sophomore year at Montana State had ended to announce that she was subleasing an apartment for the summer.

"An apartment? But you have a perfectly good room here!" her mother had exclaimed.

Which was true. But Milly was tired of living in her old room like she was still a child. She hadn't even gone away to school and lived in the dorms like her friends. She'd just commuted over the pass every day from her parents' house in Livingston.

"It's easier that way," her father had said. "Cheaper, too."

And of course, he was right. She didn't have to pay for housing, and she could continue to work in the small family grocery store where she'd been working since she could barely see above the counter.

She would, of course, continue to help this summer, too. But she wasn't going to live at home. So when her friend, Alexis, whose father did something cinematographic in Hollywood but had a bolt hole apartment in Livingston, offered to share said apartment with Milly for the summer, Milly couldn't help but say yes.

She'd only moved in three days ago, but already she felt more grown-up, more alive, more daring.

That was probably why she'd let Alexis drag her to the rodeo.

But she'd still had one foot in her old life, because she'd let her sister, Dori, talk her into taking her two-year-old nephew, Jacob, with her.

"He needs to see what real men do," Dori had said. She was a single mom—the single dad having taken off before Jake was born and never come back—and she wanted Jake to know that men were different than women.

"He knows," Milly said. There was no way on earth Jake could mistake her father's judgmental, curt masculine behavior for that of the rest of the long-suffering, compassionate members of the Malone family.

"Please?" Dori said. "I just need a little space."

Milly understood that, and felt instant sympathy. She knew how hard Dori worked to keep the wolf from the door and her father from saying, "I told you so."

"Okay," she'd said. In fact, she thought taking Jake would be a good idea. It would give her a reason for going, if anyone asked. She would just say she was taking her nephew.

She didn't want people thinking she was there to snag a cowboy like Alexis was!

So why on earth was she bringing one home?

Well, that was complicated.

It was a little bit guilt for having insulted this particular one by telling her nephew that he wasn't a real cowboy. It was a little bit concern because he really did have a lean, hungry look that had almost as much to do with food as it did interest in the opposite sex. It wouldn't hurt to give him a meal, Milly rationalized.

And it would prove that her mother was wrong. Carole Malone was sure Milly was going to use bad judgment when it came to men. She knew Milly wasn't experienced enough to handle them, and she was positive that her younger daughter would do exactly what Dori had done—and get herself pregnant the minute she went out on her own.

Well, Milly wasn't Dori!

She never had been Dori. Dori had always been rebellious and headstrong and devil-may-care. Milly had been disgustingly responsible from the word *go*.

So responsible, in fact, that she was determined to feed a hungry cowboy she'd just met.

And if she had any other interest in him, well, she wasn't ready to acknowledge it. Yet.

So she let him buy her a Coke and lead her outside. They wandered past the parked cars toward the pasture that bumped up against the foothills. Milly sipped her drink slowly, relishing the moment, just looking around, registering everything, committing it to memory, not speaking.

Cash seemed content just to look, too. But a sidelong glance at him told her he wasn't looking at what he could see of the mountains and the foothills and the valley in the moonlight. He was looking at her.

Milly jerked her gaze away.

The full moon was turning the last of last winter's snow into narrow silver streaks where it still clung to the Crazy Mountains. It was a scene Milly saw every day of her life. Normally she barely noticed.

Tonight she did. Tonight the mountains looked mysterious. The moon looked romantic, like the sort that hung over the scene in a movie where the man put his arm around the girl and drew her close. The scene where he fit his body to her and tipped her chin up and—

Whoa! Hold on a minute! You've only met this guy, she warned herself.

But even so, her heart beat a little bit faster, and she

sipped her drink a little more quickly. Her knuckles were white as she gripped the can. Out of the corner of her eye, she watched her cowboy.

Out of the corner of his eye, she could tell he still watched her.

She wished she knew what other girls talked about when they picked up men. Dori seemed to have been born knowing what to talk about. Not Milly. Milly thought sometimes she ought to take a course in conversational English!

"Just jump in," Dori once told her after a disastrous prom date. "Talk. They'll listen. They don't bite." Then she'd giggled. "Much."

Milly remembered her cheeks turning a much brighter pink than Dori's at that remark. She was pretty sure they were turning pink even now as she thought it. She was cursed with fair skin that blushed at every opportunity. Her father said she looked like his mother, "a wild Irish rose."

Her father was poetic—for a grocer. And straitlaced.

He wouldn't approve of her cowboy. And he certainly wouldn't have approved of her turning down Cash Callahan's offer of a second Coke, countering with an offer to cook him a meal instead.

"I'd be happy to do it," she said quickly, trying to get past her awkwardness as fast as possible, "if you'd like one."

"Like one?" Cash's brows hiked up a notch. Then he rubbed his flat belly and grinned his wonderful cowboy grin. "Lead me to it."

So she did.

She took him home. She didn't worry that Alexis would be there. She knew the local cowboy Alexis had her sights set on, and she didn't doubt that Alexis would be successful in her quest.

"I'll see you tomorrow," Alexis had said when they'd separated at the door of the dance hall after the rodeo.

"But—"

"I won't need a ride. And don't wait up." Then, waggling her fingers at Milly, she'd set off after the local bull rider she'd had her eye on.

Milly had looked at Jake, dozing in her arms, and probably would have gone home right then, but Dori suddenly appeared to take him off her hands.

"I would have brought him home," Milly had protested.

"I know. But I had my break," Dori told her. "I didn't expect you to keep him all night. Besides, there are plenty of better prospects here than a two-year-old." She'd surveyed the sea of dancing and grinning cowboys and wannabes, then given her little sister a shove. "Enjoy."

Milly hadn't enjoyed—until she'd set eyes on the cowboy she'd insulted earlier that evening. Then she'd felt compelled to go up to him and apologize, to make amends for causing him discomfort.

She hadn't counted on enjoying her conversation with him. But then he'd grinned...and explained...and she'd seen him as a person.

And, well, that was when she'd sort of...let herself get carried away.

And now he was sitting next to her as she drove home!

What have you done, you idiot? she asked herself, shivering slightly in response to the heat that seemed to emanate from him, though he sat a respectable six inches away.

Nothing, she answered just as promptly. She hadn't done anything—except *finally* take a step toward having her own life.

Are you sure you can trust him? She could almost hear her mother asking the words.

Well, no. She hadn't exactly known him long enough for that. But Gladys Deal, the older lady who lived downstairs, would undoubtedly be keeping an eye on things. Gladys lived other people's lives for them. It was her only means of entertainment. And it was quite enough. She even found Alexis's life a bit more than she could handle.

She had told Milly just yesterday that it was "restful" having her around.

If ever there was a goad for a nineteen-year-old woman to do something about her life, being told she was restful had to be it!

I'm all done being restful, she said silently to Gladys's twitching curtains as she pulled up in front of the apartment. Then she turned to Cash and pasted on her very best confident-woman-in-charge-of-her-own-destiny smile. "We're home."

Three

It was easy.

Too easy.

Of course Cash had had girls invite him home with them before. He'd had them bat their eyelashes and smile seductively and wiggle their hips when they led the way more times than he could recall.

But Milly Malone hadn't really done any of that.

She'd turned down his offer of a second Coke, then countered it with her own offer—of a meal.

He'd been offered meals before—that hadn't turned out to be only meals, either. But Milly hadn't batted her lashes once. And her smile had seemed more nervous than seductive.

Still, it had worked.

He'd said yes. And not so much for the meal. For once in his adult life he didn't feel as if he could eat a two-pound T-bone in thirty seconds flat. In fact, he didn't really care if she fed him at all. He just wanted to spend some more time with Milly Malone.

And maybe not entirely for the sex, either, though he sure as hell wasn't going to say no when the time came. Still, there was more to it than that.

No girl had ever taken him to task for swearing before, then worried about a horse stepping on him and then looked as if it was her personal responsibility to fatten him up!

It made him feel sort of warm inside. Cared for. He liked that. He liked her.

He'd like to know her better.

He figured he had the night to get to do it.

That's what nights were for, weren't they? And Rod could have the truck. He'd made a point of finding him and telling him so before they left. "Pick me up in the morning," he'd said, and he'd given him the address that Milly gave him.

He didn't ask himself what he'd do if she threw him out before then. She wouldn't throw him out. Cash knew that. He was an expert on such things.

How much of all this Milly herself realized when they set out for her place, he didn't know. But he figured that, innocent as she seemed, she must know the score. She wouldn't have invited him home otherwise, would she?

He didn't know about that. But the women he'd met since he'd started going down the road had taught him one thing that rodeo hadn't—that slow was always sure and if he just remembered that, he'd end up where he wanted to go.

"Looks like a nice place," he said as he followed her up the stairs.

"It's not mine, really." She looked back at him. "It belongs to my friend. I'm just sharing it with her for the summer. I just moved in a few days ago."

"From where?"

"My parents'." She shot him a quick smile as she unlocked the door.

Instinctively Cash looked over his shoulder. "Your parents?"

Milly nodded. "They live across the river." She stepped back and ushered him in. "My dad owns a grocery store in town."

"Ah." He grinned. "Bet you don't go hungry, then."

Milly laughed. "No. I never have." She hung her jacket on a hook in the kitchen. "And you won't, either, tonight. What would you like?"

Cash shrugged off his jacket and hung it next to hers, then hung his hat beside it. "Whatever you've got. Reckon I could eat most anything. But you don't have to feed me," he added conscientiously. "I'm not starvin'. I just...wanted to come with you."

Milly, halfway to the refrigerator, stopped abruptly and turned her head to look at him, her eyes wide, then suddenly wary, like a deer caught in headlights.

He gave her a lopsided grin meant to be reassuring. "What's wrong with that? You're nice," he said simply. "I like you."

"You don't know me."

"Not yet," he agreed. "But I'm tryin' to. I know you don't like swearin'."

She blushed a little. "I had Jake with me," she explained. "My nephew."

"Ah." He grinned again and looked around. "I wondered where you'd stashed the kid."

"He belongs to my sister. She's raising him by herself and she...wanted him to see men in action."

"But not swearing." Cash grinned.

She colored just a little. "That was my idea," Milly admitted.

"You were right. I shouldn't've said it."

"You'd nearly been stepped on! You were frightened!"

"I was not!" Cash was affronted at the very idea. "I was mad 'cause I wasn't gonna win anything!"

"Oh." Milly looked like she was digesting that.

"I didn't mind that you told me off for swearin'," he said quickly. "Eventually," he added. Then, "Nobody ever has. And not a lot of women have ever cared if a bronc stepped on me, either, even if you did think I was scared."

"Sorry," Milly said.

Cash shrugged. "Just so's you know, I wasn't. But I figure it makes you pretty special for carin'. So that's why I'm here. No meal. No ulterior motives." He spread his hands and did his best to look like he hadn't just taken off a black hat.

Milly just looked at him, assessing, weighing, concluding. And then, finally, a slow happy smile dawned on her face. "Good."

Cash blinked. *Good?*

She was *glad?* She didn't *want* him to have ulterior motives? She was going to be happy just to cook him a meal?

"But I'll make you a meal, anyway," she said. "Eggs and bacon and toast?" Milly turned away to poke her head into the refrigerator. "Hash browns with cheese?"

Cash couldn't say no. His stomach was always willing. "Sounds good."

Milly got out the bacon and the eggs. She got out potatoes and cheese and bread. She moved with the easy efficiency of someone completely at home in the kitchen. Cash could burn himself boiling water. He leaned against the counter that separated the kitchen from the living room-dining room and watched. It wasn't just her efficiency he admired. He liked the gentle curves of her body, the way her breasts lifted when she reached up to get a plate out of the cupboard, the inch of bare midriff he glimpsed when her shirt pulled out of her jeans. He liked her rounded bottom and imagined how it would feel snug against him.

Not the way to go slow, he reminded himself. He cleared his throat.

"You lived in Livingston all your life?"

"Forever. My whole family has been here forever," she said with a smile. "My great-grandparents came from Illinois a hundred years ago. Great-grandpa started working for some mercantile store, then he bought a place of his own. A grocery. He ran it. My grandfather ran it. Now it's my dad's. As soon as we kids were able to see over the counter, we started working there, too. I still do when I'm not at school."

"You're in school?"

"Montana State. I just finished my sophomore year."

"A kid," Cash said with a grin, relieved at least that she didn't mean high school! He wasn't into cradle snatching.

"I'm almost twenty," she said.

His tongue traced a circle on the inside of his cheek. "Ancient."

"How old are you?"

"Twenty-four." Lately, with all his aches and pains when he got up in the morning, eighty-four felt closer to the truth.

"That's pretty old, all right," Milly said, nodding seriously as she laid out slices of bacon in the frying pan.

Cash scowled until he saw that, despite her grave face, there was a twinkle in her eyes. "I've been around," he admitted.

"I haven't."

"You've been to Bozeman."

She laughed. "Yes, and Billings. And once I went as far as Denver." She sighed as she cracked the eggs into a bowl. "I liked Denver."

"Me, too. Especially the stock show in January. I won

there three years ago.'' It was one of the better wins in his career so far, so he reckoned he was allowed to brag a little.

"Won?"

"The saddle bronc title. At the rodeo," he explained when she looked blank.

"Oh. Of course." Her laugh was self-conscious. "Tonight was the first time I've ever been to a rodeo."

"Ever?" Cash was shocked.

Milly shrugged. "My father's a grocer, not a rancher."

"But still! This is Montana."

"We didn't ever go. He's not exactly...Western. And he's not very big on, um, cowboys."

There were people like that, people who judged you before they met you. It wasn't Milly's fault her father was one of them. "His loss," he said lightly.

Milly looked almost sad. "Yes," she agreed, her voice quiet. She took a deep breath and let it out slowly, then raised her eyes and smiled at him. "Not mine," she said with equally quiet firmness.

Their eyes met. Cash felt the same almost primal attraction he'd felt the first time he'd looked at her. His mouth was as dry as dirt, his palms as damp as a kid's.

And then Milly said, "The bacon's burning!" and turned back to take care of it, just as if she hadn't left Cash on fire as well.

It was okay, he told himself. He needed a little breathing space. Milly didn't look like the type who'd take to being swept off her feet. *Cool it,* he told himself, and hoped to hell he could.

"What about you? Where are you from?" she asked, her attention on the bacon.

Cash rubbed his palms against the sides of his jeans. "Oklahoma. That's where I was born, anyhow. We moved around quite a bit."

An understatement if there ever was one. Cash had been

to a dozen schools in a dozen years. Stability was not his old man's long suit. According to Len Callahan there was always going to be a better job or greener grass or a finer place just the other side of the river or the state line or the rainbow.

There never had been. But it hadn't stopped the old man from dragging them all over the Southwest looking. The most Cash could say was that, now that he was grown and his brothers and sister had all taken off, too, his old man had settled some. The folks had bought a little place in Texas about three years back, and they were still there—as long as Cash remembered them being anywhere.

There was sure no multi-generational allegiance to anything like the grocery store Milly's family seemed attached to.

"How long you had this store, anyway?" he asked.

"Since 1903."

It boggled Cash's mind. He shook his head. "In my line of work, eight seconds is a long time," he said wonderingly.

"In your line of work it definitely is." Milly started grating potatoes. "How long have you ridden broncs?"

He told her about the first time he'd ever ridden—on a dare from his best friend when they were twelve. "Plowed the pasture with my forehead," he said with a wry grin.

Milly winced, then said admiringly, "But you stuck with it."

"Oh, yeah. I liked it. Still do. There isn't anything I've ever liked better." He warmed to the topic, basking in her interest. Cash wasn't used to talking about himself quite so much. Rod and Pete knew all there was to know about him and had for years. When you traveled day in and day out with the same guys, they knew you better than they knew their own mothers.

But nobody else knew him well. Not even the girls who

clamored around him after the rodeos. Especially not them. They rarely seemed to want to. All that interested them was what was below his belt buckle.

Usually that was about all he cared about, too. But he didn't mind telling Milly more. She seemed genuinely interested. Whenever he stopped for a breath, she asked another question and he talked on. He was still talking—telling her about his greatest triumph, a win at Cheyenne that just happened to fall on his twentieth birthday—when she set the plate on the table and gestured for him to dig in.

He did. She sat down across from him, sipping a cup of coffee and smiling at him. Cash smiled back and, between bites, he asked about her.

She told him about the two years she'd spent at Montana State so far. She told him about her family—the sister and nephew and an older brother. Then she talked about her accounting classes, about her plans for the future.

"I won't stay here," she said firmly. "I'm going to see the world." There was an eager light in her eyes that made him smile.

"Good idea," he said. "Everybody ought to."

"I'm going to start at my brother's," she told him. "Deke lives in New Mexico."

He was part cowboy, part photographer, she told him. When Cash heard his name, he said he thought he remembered seeing some of Deke Malone's work displayed at Prescott or maybe it was Albuquerque.

Milly nodded eagerly. "Both probably. He's very good."

From what Cash could remember, that was true enough.

"And my sister writes," Milly told him. "She does wonderful children's stories."

"Books?"

"She'd like to. She has, actually, but she never sends

them in. She doesn't think they're good enough. They are, though," Milly said stoutly. "They're wonderful."

Cash believed her. There was a sincerity about Milly when she spoke of her family that defied you *not* to believe her. "How 'bout you?" he asked. "What do you do?"

"I paint," Milly said.

His brows lifted. He glanced around the room, but didn't see anything beyond the general travel poster decor.

"Walls," she added with an impish grin. "No, really," she said when he started to protest. "I don't do anything. They're the creative ones, Deke and Dori. I'm not. I'm the audience. I sit on the sidelines and cheer. Somebody's got to do it." She shrugged.

Cash looked at her closely, trying to detect a hint of bitterness, some glimmer in her gaze that betrayed her dissatisfaction. But she seemed totally sincere.

He had the fleeting feeling that he wouldn't mind having her sitting on the sidelines cheering for him. He wondered if her family knew how lucky they were.

"Nobody else sits on the sidelines?"

"My mother, I guess," Milly said. "She's always been very supportive of all of us."

"Not your dad?"

"Dad is…Dad. He doesn't cheer, he just tells us what to do."

There was something in her voice that made Cash say, "But you don't?"

"*I* do," Milly said. She made a face. "I've always done everything he said." She sounded disgusted.

"But not your brother and sister?"

"Not…always." She ran her tongue over her lips and didn't say anything else.

Cash didn't probe. It wasn't any of his business. *Milly* wasn't any of his business, he reminded himself. He didn't usually ask questions like this. Of course, he didn't usually just sit at some girl's kitchen table and do nothing but talk!

But he didn't mind talking with Milly. Still, it wouldn't do to get *too* interested. He finished off the eggs she'd put in front of him and mopped up the yolk with a piece of toast. "This is awful good."

She beamed. "Would you like more? How about more coffee?"

"Just coffee, thanks." He settled back in his chair and pushed his empty plate away. He was stuffed, sated. Sleepy. His myriad aches and pains seemed to have receded into a vague fog of faint discomfort. Nothing unmanageable. He folded his hands across his flat belly and watched while Milly carried his plate to the sink, then topped off his coffee mug.

Again he was impressed by her easy efficiency. Her movements were fluid, graceful. She handled the kitchen the way he handled a bronc. But she was definitely prettier to watch. She reached up to put away the coffee, and the hem of her shirt lifted again and he got another glimpse of that inch or two of bare skin.

Cash had seen his share of naked female flesh. In wholesale quantities it didn't tantalize him anywhere near as much as these few inches of Milly did. He swallowed and shrugged into the seat of the chair trying to get a little more room in his Wranglers.

He'd eaten too damn much. That was why they were suddenly so tight.

Uh-huh.

"Lemme help you with that," he said, surging to his feet, adjusting his jeans as he did so. He stepped forward and just happened to reach around to help her with the plates as she turned around. Directly into—against—his chest. Her breasts brushed his ribs.

He sucked in a quick, sharp breath. And winced badly.

"What's wrong?" Milly spun out of the way.

Cash braced himself against the counter with his palms and dredged up a rueful grin to mask the lingering pain. "Nothin'. It's just those damn...er, darn...ribs again."

"Did I hurt you?"

He shook his head and straightened up slowly. "Of course not. I just...turned wrong. I forget sometimes and do somethin' stupid, and then they let me know."

He should have put that damned bandage back on right after his ride. But at the time, he'd figured he could last until he got back to Pete's house.

He hadn't figured it would be long.

He hadn't counted on Milly.

"I got a bandage I'm supposed to wrap 'em with, but I didn't put it on after my ride."

"Do you have it with you?"

"In my rigging bag."

"I'll help you put it on."

He blinked in astonishment. But as he did so, he realized that her offer was perfectly innocent. Unpremeditated. As if she didn't have a clue what inviting him to take his shirt off could lead to.

She gave him an eager, helpful smile, and Cash—damn him for a negative role model!—couldn't set her straight.

"I'll go get it," he said, and headed out to get his rigging bag from her car.

"I used to tape Deke's ankles for him when he played ball," Milly said when he came back and set the bag on the floor, then hunkered down over it.

It wasn't going to be the same, but he wasn't going to tell her that. Instead he gave her a quick reassuring grin, "Great. You're experienced then."

"Oh, yes," she said as he began opening his shirt.

Something almost sultry in her voice made him glance at her. She was looking at him with such avid interest, he felt his body heat up. He was used to taking women's clothes off before he shed his own. He'd never been the first one out of his clothes.

Hell, he almost felt like he was stripping in front of her! But hey, if it worked...

He tried to ease his shirt off without turning his shoulder or twisting and hurting his ribs.

"Let me help." And the next thing he knew she was taking his shirt off for him. She was very matter-of-fact in her movements. Her hands didn't linger. They didn't stroke him or caress.

It didn't matter. His mind was managing quite nicely with only the barest help from her; it was taking her lightest touch and turning it into a titillating experience; it was taking the feel of her warm breath on his bare skin and making it a seductive ploy.

And if her removal of his shirt got his mind working overtime—the soft play of her hands on him, once she took the elastic bandage from him and began to wrap his ribs— well, he tried not to think about that—yet.

"Do you want me to fix it so it immobilizes your arm, too?" she asked him.

Cash cleared his throat. "Er, naw. The ribs are enough. I, um, might want to use my arms."

"But your shoulder—"

"It's okay." He rolled it experimentally and couldn't help grimacing a little. "Just a little knotted up. Don't suppose you could maybe knead 'em a bit?"

It was a perfectly legitimate request. It would feel a hell of a lot better if somebody rubbed his shoulders. And if something else happened after that, he couldn't predict it with absolute certainty, could he?

"Lie down," Milly said.

Cash would have dropped where he stood, but he didn't want to appear too eager. He looked around. There was the couch, and there was the floor. The couch was probably more comfortable, but it didn't look long enough. He looked doubtfully at the hard, oak floor.

"On my bed." Milly took his hand. "Come on."

He couldn't believe it.

He wasn't having to do any work at all! But he wasn't about to argue. He followed her into her bedroom.

It was a small room. Neat and modestly adorned. "I haven't been here long enough to do much decorating," she said quickly, as if embarrassed by its Spartan decor.

"Hey, it's great." A whole lot better than the back of Rod's truck.

Cash actually found himself liking the fact that she only had a single bed. He took that to mean that she didn't habitually entertain overnight guests. Cash felt a stab of satisfaction as he sat down on the edge of the bed and looked up at her.

She smiled nervously, as if she might be realizing that she'd just invited a strange man into her bedroom.

He had no desire to frighten her. He just wanted to make love with her. So he smiled back and asked, as offhand as he could, "You mind if I take my boots off?"

She blinked, then swallowed. "Oh, no. Um, go right ahead."

Getting them off wasn't easy, given the state of his ribs. But Milly helped with that, too. And doing so seemed to make her feel less nervous, as if she were in control. Cash didn't mind.

He was embarrassed to note, though, that he had a hole in the toe of his sock. He knew Milly saw it, too. Her finger brushed his bare toe and made him jerk. But she didn't say a word, just set his boots at the foot of the bed and straightened up, then waited. The nervous look was back again.

Slowly, carefully Cash lay back and stretched out on her bed, then looked up at her. "You scared?" he asked her.

"Of course not. I've taken judo."

He gaped. "Judo?"

Her cheeks went bright red. "You know. To pro—" She stopped, as if she couldn't say the words, then said, "I didn't mean—that is, I don't think—"

A grin quirked the corner of his mouth. "You reckon you can protect yourself." If she didn't want to say it, he would say it for her.

"That's right."

"You won't have to," he promised. "You're in charge."

She smiled at him then, a wide smile, a genuine smile. "Turn over, Cash Callahan. I'll rub your shoulders."

Cash turned over. He lay on his stomach. His sock-clad feet hung over the end of the bed. He turned his head so he could see her as she stood above him.

He waited, held himself perfectly still, didn't even breathe as Milly bent and put her hands on his shoulders. Her fingers moved, squeezed lightly, her thumbs pressed the sensitive cords of his neck, made his spine ripple.

A tremor ran through him. A soft moan escaped him.

Milly jerked back. "Am I hurting you?"

"No!" God, no! It felt wonderful. "It's fine. Keep going."

She kneaded his shoulders again. And again. She stroked and pushed. Loosened the knots. Rubbed the pads of her thumbs against the nape of his neck, untying knots there, too, that he didn't even know he had.

"'S wonderful," he mumbled.

"Good. Move over."

He jerked. "What?"

"So I can sit next to you," she explained. "It'll be easier. If I do it from here much longer I'll have a crick in *my* back."

He grinned. "I'd rub it for you."

"Nice of you." He heard the smile in her voice. He didn't see it. He'd shut his eyes.

It felt better than wonderful, the way her hands were moving rhythmically on his shoulders and neck. It felt like the best thing that had ever happened to him. He yawned and flexed his shoulders. "More," he muttered when her hands faltered for a moment.

"Just getting settled," she said. The bed shifted a little more. Her hip pressed against his side. He smiled.

Milly went on kneading. And kneading. "How's that?"

Cash let out a soft sigh. "Fantastic. Dunno why you're working in a grocery store. Or taking accounting. You ought to give back rubs for a living."

She laughed. He liked her laugh. It was soft and warm and intimate.

Intimate was good. He was definitely in favor of *intimate*, he thought muzzily. In fact he intended to get intimate with her real soon.... Just as soon as she got all these knots out of his neck and back.... Just as soon as he got her clothes off....

Just as soon as...

He was asleep.

She'd actually put him to sleep.

There was finally a man in her bed—which Alexis had been assuring her for months was absolutely necessary to her well-being—and he was out like a light.

Milly shook her head, but kept up her soft, rhythmic movements on his back as she looked down at Cash Callahan and smiled.

He looked exhausted. Beaten. And beautiful at the same time.

She'd thought that the moment she saw him scrambling over the fence. It had been like a blow to the solar plexus—the sudden intense attraction she'd felt, the realization that she really wasn't as immune as she'd always thought she must be to stark masculine attraction.

It had never hit her before. She'd never been able to understand what had driven Dori to go to bed with Jake's father.

Now—for the very first time—she did.

And she knew she might actually have made love with Cash Callahan—if he'd managed to stay awake!

She supposed she ought to be chagrined or questioning her own sex appeal. She could just imagine what Alexis would say. Not that she had any intention of telling her! What happened here—or hadn't happened here—tonight was between her and Cash Callahan.

Someday she might regret that nothing had.

But then again, someday she might be glad. She knew that innocence wasn't exactly an "in-thing" these days. Sometimes she felt like a walking, talking anachronism. But she had seen what Dori went through. She had seen the pain of single motherhood, of love unrequited, of getting in too deep, too soon. It scared her.

Cash, awake, scared her a little, too.

But asleep, he was the most beautiful, the most wonderful, the most tempting thing she'd ever seen.

She wanted just to sit here and look at him. To touch him. She touched him again now.

He shifted slightly in his sleep. His one good arm came up to rest on her knee. Now *he* was touching her. She lifted her hand from his back and traced his fingers with hers.

She liked his hands. They looked strong even in repose. They were hard and callused. Not grocer's hands. Nothing at all like her father's.

Cash wasn't like her father. She understood that at once. He had no steady job. No determined focus on responsibility. No roots.

He was, she feared, very much like the man who had left Dori behind.

But maybe not. It might be wrong to tar him with the same brush without giving him a chance to show her who he really was. She certainly wanted to know who he really was.

She didn't suppose she would get to find out. She imagined he'd be here tonight and gone tomorrow—that he would be no more than a fleeting moment in her otherwise steady, humdrum life.

Well, so be it.

At least she had tonight.

She eased herself gently off the bed, careful not to wake him. Then she padded out into the living room. She looked at his rigging bag lying open by the door. It looked out of place—and yet somehow, exactly right. As if it belonged—as if *he* belonged. To her.

She didn't let herself think about that. Instead she shut off the lights and went back into the bedroom.

Cash hadn't moved.

She wondered if propriety required that she sleep in Alexis's room. Certainly her mother and father would think it did. But propriety wasn't the topmost thing on her mind tonight. She wanted to stay here.

She left the small lamp on so she could look her fill at him and so it wouldn't seem quite so intimate if he woke up and wondered where he was or—horror of horrors—who *she* was! Then she crossed the room to the bed.

She couldn't bring herself to actually lie down next to him. It wasn't just propriety. It was presumption that stopped her. She didn't want him thinking she was trying to take advantage of him!

Still, she couldn't just stand there all night like some ridiculous guardian angel. She could sit beside him on the

bed. That would be proper enough, and no more presumptuous than giving him the back rub had been.

Carefully Milly eased herself onto it next to him. His
nose pressed against her thigh. His hair brushed her jean-
clad hip. He murmured in his sleep. She reached out a
tentative hand and brushed it across his hair.

It was as soft as Jake's. She smiled and relaxed a little,
brushing her hand over it again.

Cash muttered. And then his arm came up and wrapped
around her, and he hauled her down into his embrace!

For an instant Milly stiffened, resisted—then felt her re-
sistance fail. Like she was meant to be there, she slid down
next to him and felt the hard, warm length of his body
against hers, felt the rasp of his day-old whiskery cheek on
her smooth one. It was wonderful. It was astonishing. It
was so...so...right!

And then he kissed her.

It was a long kiss, a drugging kiss. A tantalizing kiss. A
kiss of the sort that Milly had only imagined existed. If
she'd been standing, it would have knocked her over.

She enjoyed it. She got into it. She opened her mouth
tentatively, hesitantly. Then with increasing enthusiasm she
kissed him back. She felt hot. She felt hungry. She felt
everything that she'd only been able to guess that Dori felt.

And then Cash rolled onto his back and began to snore.

Four

The deep insistent *ooo-gah* of the horn woke him.

That and the tendril of hair tickling his nose.

Cash blinked, then opened his eyes and stared at the girl asleep on the bed beside him. What the—?

He gave himself a little shake. It hurt. *He* hurt.

But he also remembered...the dance...Milly...the back rub...the—

No, damn it, he didn't remember that! Wished he could. Tried to. But couldn't.

Had he? Had *they*?

She lay curled on her side against him, her lips slightly parted. They looked kissed.

Hell, he couldn't even remember *kissing* her!

And she was still dressed. She didn't even have a button of her shirt undone! Cash's hand explored his own torso. Bare except for the bandage. His hand slid lower and encountered his belt, still buckled.

He groaned.

Another deep *ooo-gah* reverberated outside. Annoying. Irritating. Demanding. Familiar.

Kind of like the horn on Rod's truck.

Oh, God.

Cash eased himself away from Milly and sat up. He was stiff, moving slowly, not wanting to do this at all. And yet—

Another impatient *ooo-gah*.

He hauled himself out of the bed.

Milly's eyes opened, too, wide and wondering. She looked rumpled and cuddly and—

Another *ooo-gah*.

Damn. He stumbled out into the living room and pushed back the curtain. Rod saw him and gave a yell.

"Hurry up! We gotta be in Wolf Point by two!"

Cash gave a wave of his hand in acknowledgment and let the curtain fall again.

"What is it?" Milly had followed him out of the bedroom and stood looking at him. Her hair was tangled around her face and her shirttails were untucked.

At least he'd got *that* far, Cash thought, disgusted with himself.

Or maybe he hadn't.

Maybe the night's sleep had untucked them for her. Cripes, how could he have just conked out like that? He smothered a groan.

"It's my buddies," he said ruefully. "I gotta go."

"Go?" There was a pause, then. "Of course. Go." She looked slightly sad, totally resigned.

Cash didn't feel resigned. He felt cheated.

He'd spent the night with Milly Malone, for crying out loud, and all he had to show for it were some nicely bandaged ribs!

The horn sounded again.

He cursed under his breath, then, remembering, muttered, "Sorry."

"I don't suppose you all have time for breakfast?"

He shook his head. "We don't have time for breakfast." He glanced at his watch and winced. They were going to have to drive like the proverbial bat out of hell if he stopped long enough to pull on his shirt! He took three strides back toward the bedroom to get it.

Milly watched. "Um, well," she began as he brushed past her, "it was…nice meeting you."

"Wasn't it?" Cash said bitterly, then raked a hand through his rumpled hair and apologized again. "This isn't how I planned it."

Her brows lifted. "Planned it?"

"I mean—I didn't expect to just eat your food and fall asleep on your bed!" He could feel hot blood coursing into his face. He felt like seven kinds of idiot. He pulled his shirt on and began to do it up.

"It's all right," she said quietly. "I didn't mind."

"I did." They stared at each other. Seconds passed. Cash heard footsteps pounding up the steps, and then there was a loud hammering on the front door.

"Damn it!" He finished buttoning his shirt and jammed it into his jeans. "Cut that out!" he yelled. "I'm comin' as fast as I can!"

Milly handed him his boots, and as he yanked them on, she went to answer the door.

Pete stood there, grinning self-consciously. "Don't mean to interrupt anything, um, real personal," he said to Milly apologetically, then he looked past her at Cash and went on, "but we gotta haul a—um, ourselves outa here!"

"I told you I'm comin'," Cash said. "Hold your horses."

"I will," Pete said. "They won't." At the rodeo he meant.

Cash zipped up his rigging bag, scowling. Pete, looking at Milly, touched his fingers to the brim of his hat. "Plea-sure meetin' you, miss."

"You, too," Milly said faintly. She watched him head back downstairs, then turned to Cash.

He hoisted the bag and settled his hat on his head. He didn't know what to say other than "I wish..."

"Yes." She smiled. "Me, too." The words were guile-less. Sincere. They made him ache. And desire.

He deserved to ache, damn it! And he was just going to have to go on desiring because Rod hit the horn again. Twice.

Milly smiled. "Bye."

"Bye." His voice was hoarse. He stepped forward and kissed her.

It was not a good idea. The desperation in it should have sent her running. The desire in it should have scared her to death. Instead she put her arms around him and hugged him hard!

To Cash the hug felt more intimate than any kiss. It spoke less of sex than of love. Love? Naw, it couldn't! He didn't do *love*. Wouldn't know how if he wanted to—which he didn't.

It scared him to death.

It tempted him, too.

Then, as quickly as she had embraced him, Milly stepped back. "I'm sorry. I'll hurt you. Hurt your ribs."

"No." And it was the truth. She'd been gentle with him. They stared at each other.

"Cash! For cryin' out loud!" The voice bellowing out-side broke the connection.

"Gotta go," Cash said, though his boots still wouldn't move.

"Yes. You do." Milly reached out a hand and touched

his for an instant. Then she dropped it again and gave him a smile. "Go on."

"You had a man here? Overnight?" Alexis looked dumbfounded. Then her eyes got big and sparkly, and she squealed and giggled and grabbed Milly by the shoulders and jumped up and down. "I knew it! I knew you had some wild oats to sow!"

Milly ran her tongue over her lips. "It wasn't quite like that, Alexis."

But Alexis wasn't listening. "Which one was he? The one with the cute butt? Oh, they all had cute butts! Was he the cute one in the blue and purple shirt? Or the one in black and white stripes?"

Milly shook her head. Cash's shirt had been red. Plain red. Vibrant red. Eye-catching red. Like Cash. And yes, she'd noticed his butt, and she'd approved.

Still, she couldn't quite believe he'd been here. Even though she—and Gladys downstairs—had watched the battered blue truck until it disappeared around the corner, Milly felt, once Cash was gone, as if she'd imagined the whole thing.

It was so unlikely that she, Millicent Margaret Malone, virgin grocery clerk and college student, had spent the night in a cowboy's arms.

Who'da thunk it? as her sister Dori would say.

Well, Dori wouldn't, that was certain. But Alexis seemed to.

She was still giggling and dancing around the living room. "What was his name? What event was he in? Did you meet him at the dance? How did you ever get him to come back with you? You never say peep to anyone."

"He was, um, the one who climbed over the fence and swore."

Alexis gaped. "The one you said..." She covered her

mouth with her hand. Then she burst out laughing. "Well, I guess you had something to talk about, didn't you?"

"Sort of." Milly's fingers knotted. "He was very nice."

Alexis gave her a knowing grin. "I'll bet."

"Not like that!"

Alexis's face fell. "No? Oh, what a shame."

"I mean we didn't—" Milly broke off. She didn't want to just come right out and *say* that nothing had happened. Except, knowing her, Alexis probably knew that, anyway. Still…it wasn't something you just went around admitting.

"He had cracked ribs," she said without thinking.

"And did you bandage them?" Alexis asked sweetly.

Milly nodded.

"Volunteered, I bet."

"It would have been hard for him to do them himself."

"Of course it would." Alexis gave her a butter-wouldn't-melt-in-my-mouth smile. "And then I bet you gave him a back rub."

"How did you know?"

Alexis rolled her eyes. "You're a natural. I can't believe this. My God, Milly, you've been hiding under a bushel basket for how many years? Men everywhere have been missing out and—"

"Stop it! He is *not* men everywhere! He was just one man. Cash! And I wouldn't do it for just any man, either," Milly said hotly.

Alexis stared at her. "Ohmigod."

Milly scowled. "What's that supposed to mean?"

"It means you're in love with him."

"Of course I'm not in love with him! I barely know him. I just met him!"

"Is he coming back?"

"Probably not." Oddly, having to say the words hurt. Maybe there was a tiny bit of truth to what Alexis had said.

No, of course there wasn't! Milly wasn't in love with Cash Callahan. A woman didn't fall in love overnight.

Did she?

What Milly knew about love—real love—would have filled a thimble with about a finger's worth of room left over.

"So you're saying it was a one-night stand, then?" Alexis followed Milly into her bedroom. Fortunately she had straightened the bed after Cash left, though she hadn't been able to bring herself to fluff up her pillow, the pillow Cash had used. If you looked closely you could still see the indentation where his head had lain. Milly brushed her fingers lightly over it now.

"It was not a one-night stand," she said sharply.

Alexis beamed. "I didn't think so! Well, I had a good time with *my* cowboy, too. In fact, I'm meeting Tony for a picnic later. Gotta grab a shower now." She waggled her fingers at Milly, then tripped down the hall and shut herself in the bathroom.

Milly stood unmoving, contemplating the empty afternoon that stretched before her—contemplating life after Cash.

It wasn't any big deal.

It might not have been a one-night stand, but apparently it had been a one-off. Milly assured herself that she'd always known that. So what, if in the first week or so after Cash had blown through her life, she might have had a few fairy-tale daydreams in which he came back and swept her off her feet. When days turned into weeks and weeks into a month, she adjusted.

By the middle of August, she no longer reached for the phone hopefully every time it rang. By the end of the month, she didn't come home from the grocery store every evening and look around the street to see if there just might be a blue truck somewhere in the vicinity—a blue truck that had seen better days and had a dent all along the passenger side.

By the first of September she had pretty much forgotten what he looked like. She scarcely remembered the tiny mole by his left ear. And she had almost forgotten those thirteen stitches in his jaw. He wouldn't have those anymore anyway, so there was certainly no point in remembering them.

She wasn't even sure anymore if his sideburns stopped just below the top of his ear or crept down half an inch or so.

She wasn't even staring off into space the way she did the week right after the rodeo. She almost never mismarked the canned goods anymore. And if her father was short-tempered with her, it was because he was cranky, not because she was woolgathering when she ought to be sorting through the produce for fruit that was beginning to turn.

She was fine. Perfectly fine.

But she kept turning down dates with very nice men.

Dori didn't understand it. "Why?" she asked, when she heard Milly turn down an invitation to the Sweet Pea Festival with Tom Rosser.

"Are you out of your mind?" she demanded when a week later she heard her sister decline a chance to go to Billings to a concert with Jeff Conover.

"You're crazy," she said when Milly said "no, thanks" to a chance to go to a movie with Mike Dutton.

"You're not waiting on that cowboy, are you?" she asked, eyeing Milly narrowly across the kitchen of their parents' house.

Milly shrugged. She'd never been much good at lying. And if she wasn't exactly "waiting for" Cash, she wasn't all that eager to go out with anyone else, either.

"You're insane if you are," Dori said frankly. "You'll never see him again."

"She's right," said Milly's mother, Carole.

It was the first thing Dori and her mother had agreed on in years.

"They never settle down," she went on firmly. "They're here today, gone tomorrow. Undependable, every last one." Carole Malone thumped the frying pan she was drying down on the stove for emphasis.

Dori looked at Milly and raised her eyebrows. "Do we have a little experience talking here?" she asked her mother.

Carole rounded on her daughter. "Yours, not mine," she said flatly.

Dori bristled, and Milly, out of habit, stepped between them.

"I'm not 'waiting,' Mom," she said, placating things as she always did. "I just...don't care."

"Well, you ought to care," Carole said sharply. "If you don't start caring pretty soon, you're going to be an old maid. What about young Ted Weston? What was wrong with the Conover boy? I can't believe you said no to Mike Dutton. He's gorgeous."

One by one she managed to tick off all the boys who'd ever asked Milly for a date, all the boys in whom Milly had been interested—or had been interested in her—B.C. Before Cash.

But Milly wasn't interested in any of those boys now. Because compared to Cash, they *were* boys—not men.

Cash was a man. He'd been around, seen the world. Cash had fought a few battles in his time. You could see it in his face and in his eyes, in his broken ribs and stitched-up jaw.

But Milly didn't say any of that to her mother. She knew

that, like Jake's father, Cash was not the sort of guy who thrilled mothers. Mothers wanted their daughters to be safe.

There was nothing safe about Cash Callahan, and hearing that Milly thought of Cash as a *man*, would only make her worry.

To be honest, it wasn't entirely true. Cash wasn't exactly a man, either, come to that. He was more like an exotic species. Wild as the broncs he rode. Restless as the wind. Rootless as a tumbleweed.

More things her mother wouldn't want to hear.

So Milly kept her mouth shut. Even though she never expected to hear from him again, she had her few thin memories.

She dragged them out more often than she ought to have, and she knew it. It wasn't hard at all to lie awake at night and remember that one time his head had lain next to hers on the pillow. It was easy to call up the feeling of his arm, warm and hard around her, no trouble at all to recall the rough, scratchy feel of his whiskery cheek under her touch, the Jake-like softness of his hair against her face.

And in the darkness, when no one else could remark on her blushes or the look of longing on her face, it was all too easy to remember—and savor—the taste of Cash's lips on hers.

She was the fish that got away.

There was sure as heck no other way to explain why he kept thinking about Milly Malone.

She wasn't the prettiest girl he'd ever gone home with. She wasn't the liveliest or the friendliest or, God knew, the best in bed.

That was it, in a nutshell. God might know, but Cash *didn't!* And he wanted to.

His buddies sure thought he had.

"Had a good night, did ya?" Rod had asked when Cash

had stood by the chutes at Wolf Point and stared off into space that first afternoon.

"Um, er, yeah," Cash had lied, because he sure wasn't telling them he hadn't got anything at all! "Great," he added firmly.

Rod and Pete exchanged glances. "Lucky dog," Pete muttered.

"Cash has got the touch," Rod agreed.

But the truth was, Milly was the one with "the touch." Only moments after she'd begun rubbing his back, he'd fallen fast asleep!

Cash couldn't believe he'd dropped off that way. But it was true. If his still-zipped jeans and fastened belt buckle hadn't attested to it, the persistent ache in his loins would have.

It was that lack of fulfillment, he told himself, that nagged him as the days passed—and not the memory of his night with Milly Malone.

The ache he could take care of—and did. Desire assuaged, he should have forgotten her.

He didn't.

Cash, to whom all women—blondes, brunettes and redheads—were equally interesting and tempting, found that none of them was as interesting as Milly Malone.

He was annoyed as hell.

When he couldn't forget her, he tried to figure out why. Maybe it was because she'd given him a back rub. No other girl had ever given him a back rub. So he talked a girl in Deadwood into giving him a back rub.

But it wasn't the same.

He thought maybe it was because Milly had such sparkly green eyes. He'd never known any girl with such lively eyes. But in Oregon he met a girl whose eyes sparkled even more than Milly's, and two days later he couldn't remember her name.

So it had to be because he fell asleep before anything had happened. It *had* to be.

It was like two years ago when he'd drawn that nasty sorrel Thunderfest three times running and got tossed each time.

He'd obsessed about Thunderfest after that—thought about him, talked about him, dreamed about him—until the fourth time, when he'd ridden him to the buzzer and nailed a fourth-place seventy-five.

Thunderfest turned out not to be that memorable after all.

It would be the same with Milly Malone.

All he had to do was go back to Livingston—and prove it.

He began looking for reasons to go through Livingston. It shouldn't be that hard. It was right on Interstate 90. Thousands of cars and trucks hurtled up and down the highway everyday. But none that Cash was in.

"What the hell do you want to go up there for?" Pete asked him every time he suggested they head Livingston way.

Cash always shrugged. "Good rodeo in Kalispell," he'd say. Or, "Thought maybe we should head up to Miles City this year. You could stop in, say hello to your folks."

"Next month," Pete always said. "We can make better money in Coffeyville." Or, "Would you look at this? Good prize money in Rapid City this year!"

So they went to Coffeyville and Dodge City and Rapid City and Abilene. And the one time they got as far north as Okotoks, Alberta, they went right back down to Dillon and on to WallaWalla without even turning east.

"What the hell d'you want to go there for?" Rod and Pete took turns asking him every time he mumbled the word *Livingston*. They never remembered Milly Malone.

No reason why they should. Cash sure as shootin' didn't

talk about her! They'd never stop teasing him if he ever let on he was a little bit interested in some girl.

And he *wasn't* really interested. He was just...well...just curious.

But his curiosity was growing, and there was no telling how big it might have got if that September night, as they were heading out of Pendleton after the performance, Pete hadn't said, "You're so interested in Livingston, why don't you catch a ride with Shane?"

Cash paused, his foot halfway up into the topper of the truck. "What?"

"Nichols broke his arm last night," Pete reminded him. "He's goin' to his brother's for a little R and R. Mace lives near Elmer. I was figurin' maybe you'd want to catch a ride."

"Elmer? Where's that?" Cash asked, surprising himself by not dismissing the notion out of hand.

"Not too far from Livingston. Not far from Bozeman, either."

Cash's insides did a funny flip-flop at the thought of it. Milly lived in Livingston. She went to school in Bozeman. Both were on the interstate. It would make perfect sense if he just happened to drop in. Did he dare?

When did Cash Callahan ever *not* dare?

He grabbed his rigging bag and the duffel in which he carried the rest of his worldly belongings. "Not a bad idea. Reckon maybe I will."

He didn't know Shane Nichols well. He was a couple of years older than Cash. He'd had a run for rookie-of-the-year while Cash was still in high school, and Shane had been friends with bigshots like Noah Tanner and Taggart Jones while Cash had still been wanting to ask for their autographs!

But for all that, he was always easygoing and friendly.

And he was happy when Cash approached him about the ride.

"Matter of fact, you can drive," Shane said, tossing Cash the keys to his truck.

He didn't complain about his broken arm, but Cash knew it had to hurt. He'd seen Shane break it. The memory of the grotesquely snapped bone could still bring a cold sweat out on the back of his neck.

"Sure thing," Cash said. He liked driving, and if Shane wanted to sleep the whole trip, that was okay with him. It'd give him something to do—besides think about Milly.

What if she didn't even remember who he was?

Of course she'd remember who he was!

Still, he didn't call and say he was coming. No sense in warning her. Maybe he'd take one look and decide the memory of what might have been wasn't worth it. Maybe he'd toss Shane back his keys and take the next bus out!

He drove eight hours. Then Shane took over. He was awake, and his arm didn't hurt so much. He was ready to talk.

Cash had always known Shane was a talker. He didn't mind. He liked listening. It kept his mind off Milly Malone.

"Where do you want me to drop you?" Shane asked.

It was late afternoon. Cash had debated asking Shane to drop him in Bozeman, since Milly went to MSU there. But he wouldn't know how to find her, and he was pretty sure she'd have to turn up back at her apartment eventually. If he went there, he wouldn't miss her. "Right by the station," he said. "I'll walk from there. Sure do appreciate the ride."

"No problem. If you're still here in three weeks or so, we can head out together."

"I won't be. I'm just…visitin' a friend. Overnight is all."

"Overnight is good." Shane grinned and gave Cash a knowing wink.

Cash felt his cheeks burn. "It ain't like that." *Yet.*

Shane's grin broadened. "Whatever you say, pard." He pulled up to the curb. "Have fun." He gave Cash a quick two-finger salute and drove away.

Cash stood on the corner, rigging bag in one hand, duffel in the other, and stared in the direction of Milly's apartment.

He hoped she remembered who he was.

She wasn't there.

Didn't live there anymore. Some girl who sparkled and batted her eyelashes, and looked like she would be more than happy to let him come in and pick up where he'd left off with Milly, told him that Milly had moved out at the beginning of September.

"It was just for the summer," the girl said. "I guess she didn't tell you that?"

"I...haven't talked to her recently. I was just...passin' through an', well..." Cash gave an awkward shrug. "Don't suppose you know where I can find her."

"She's working right now. At the grocery store. Did she tell you about the grocery store?"

Cash nodded. "But I never was there. I don't even know where it is."

The girl told him, then looked doubtfully at his bags. "You on foot?"

"Yeah."

Her brows lifted. "You came to stay? With Milly?"

Cash felt heat creep into his cheeks. "Not if she don't want me," he said quickly.

The girl laughed. "That Milly! What a dark horse! And wouldn't I like to be a fly on the wall," she said speculatively. "Come on. I'll drive you. I'm Alexis, by the way."

"Pleased to meet you. I'm Cash."

"I gathered that."

She did? Had Milly mentioned him? Had she told Alexis he fell asleep? Cash devoutly hoped not.

He trailed after Alexis and slid into the passenger seat of a candy apple red Miata. It sure wasn't a car like the one Milly drove.

She didn't drive like Milly did, either. Gunning the engine and whipping out onto the street, Alexis shot him a grin. "Hang on to your hat."

He did. Literally.

When she deposited him outside the grocery store, he gave his hat a tug and Alexis a nod. "Much obliged."

But Alexis bounced out, too. "Come on," she said. "I wouldn't miss this for the world."

Cash frowned. *Miss what?* But he didn't have time to wonder. Alexis was opening the door and beckoning to him. Hefting his bags, Cash followed her in.

"Brought you a present," Alexis sang out.

Milly looked up from the checkout, spied Alexis and waved. "Present?" she said brightly. Then her gaze went past Alexis and fastened on him.

Her jaw dropped. She went white, then red.

Cash felt a foolish grin spread all over his face. Damn, she was pretty. Even prettier than he remembered. And flustered, too. No doubt now about whether or not she remembered him.

"Cash?" She sounded half hopeful, half astonished.

"Hey, darlin'." He took a step forward. "You know what they say about bad pennies, they just keep turnin' up."

"Cash!" she said again. And this time, damned if she wasn't grinning all over her face!

She stepped out from behind the counter, oblivious to

the woman whose groceries she was checking out, and started toward him.

"Well, give 'im a kiss at least," Alexis prompted.

If it was possible for Milly to blush an even deeper red, she did. She rubbed her palms against the sides of her jeans and shook her head rapidly.

Cash gave his best woeful look. "No kiss?"

And then, after a moment more of hesitation, Milly took the last step, put her arms around him and lifted her face to meet his.

Cash had kissed his share of women in twenty-four years. He'd never had a kiss quite like this. He'd had deeper kisses, hungrier kisses, sexier kisses—but he'd never been kissed with such warmth, such feeling.

It was a kiss of welcome. Of joy. Of longing.

It was more kiss than he'd counted on. He found himself gripping her arms to steady himself. The kiss went on. And on.

And when at last Milly pulled back, Cash didn't let go. He just bent his head, resting it against hers, nuzzling his face in her hair, breathing in the scent of her, letting it flood his nostrils, remembering...dreaming...wanting...

"Cash?"

"Hmm?" He drew back and looked down at her.

Milly smiled at him. "Mrs. Corbett's waiting for me to finish ringing up her groceries."

He glanced around wildly and realized that not only was Alexis smiling at them, but a middle-aged lady was tapping her foot and glancing at her watch while she waited.

Cash flushed. "Sorry."

"I'm not," Milly said with disarming honesty. Then she gave his hand a squeeze. "You're not...leaving right away?"

"Not unless you throw me out."

"No," she said quickly. "Oh, no!"

Cash grinned. "I'll just window shop in the breakfast cereal till you're finished, then."

She was busy with customers until they closed at six. Cash prowled the breakfast cereals. He read the nutritional content of countless cans. He studied the blemishes on bananas. And all the while out of the corner of his eye, he watched Milly.

He'd told himself she wouldn't be as lovely as he remembered. He was wrong. He'd promised himself he wouldn't want her as much as he thought he would. Not true. He assured himself that one night with her would be all he'd need to put her behind him. He was even beginning to have doubts about that.

But he was willing to put it to the test. Damn, he wished she'd close up the store so they could get home.

Milly's eagerness seemed to match his. She turned red every time she looked at him and caught him looking at her. She miscounted the money twice and dropped the deposit bag as she was putting the coins into it. Then she dropped the keys when she was locking up. But finally, flushed and flustered, she was done.

"I just need to drop this in the night depository at the bank."

"Lead on." Cash slung his stuff in the back of her car. She watched wordlessly, but smiled as he slid into the front seat beside her. "I can't believe you're here," she said.

"Believe it." He reached out and took her hand in his. It was a casual move, hardly sexy, yet just touching her made his body hum.

He couldn't believe how much he wanted her. He folded her hand in his while she drove them to the bank. He accompanied her into the small drop-off porch, and while she put the pouch in, he kissed her ear.

"Cash," she protested, shivering. But she didn't step

away. He smiled and pressed closer, nibbling her neck. Her fingers tightened on his. *"Cash!"*

"What?" he asked, all innocence, and watched her melt under his gaze. "You finished? Good, then let's go home."

"Home?" She looked doubtful.

Cash looked at her from beneath hooded lids. He didn't say, *To bed.* He was sure he didn't have to.

They might not have consummated their last encounter, but Milly was no fool. She had felt his body pressed against hers moments ago. She knew what he wanted. He was pretty damn sure she wanted it, too.

"Home," he repeated. If she took him home, he'd know for sure.

She took him home.

It was a small house not far from the river. Older. Low-slung. Homey. Better than an apartment. "Glad you moved." He grabbed his bags and followed her.

"I told you that was just for the summer." Milly opened the back door.

Cash came after, prepared, as soon as she shut the door, to pull her into his arms and finish what they'd started weeks ago. He stopped dead at the sight of two people sitting at the kitchen table looking at them.

"Cash," said Milly, when he stared at her, dumbfounded, "I'd like you to meet my parents."

Five

How the hell could he bed a girl who brought him home to meet her folks?

Of course the question was rhetorical anyway. Even if he'd been able to—ignoring the scruples Cash was amazed to find he had—there was no chance.

Home—her *parents'* home—was now where Milly lived.

The apartment with Alexis was a thing of the past. *Any* apartment was a thing of the past. She was back with her folks, sleeping in her old bedroom.

Cash never even got close to it.

How could he, with her parents hovering over them for the rest of the evening? All he caught was a glimpse down the hallway toward the bedrooms where she slept. Alone.

That was the one positive thing he managed to find in the circumstances. If he wasn't going to get to sleep with Milly Malone, he was marginally comforted by the fact that no other guy was, either!

Her father, Hatchet Face, looked like he'd do in any fellow who gave bedding Milly a thought.

Cash tried not to give it a thought.

He tried to downsize his expectations—to limit them to casual conversation and meat loaf for dinner—all the while hoping he had enough money to pay for a room for the night. He supposed he could call Shane and see if his older brother would mind a body on his floor.

He didn't want to face Shane's pitying looks, though. Maybe he could call Pete's folks. They might let him—

"—spend the night?"

Cash's head jerked up. He looked at Milly across the dinner table from him. "What?" He strangled on a piece of meat loaf.

"I wondered if you'd like to spend the night?" Milly gave him a hopeful smile. "We have plenty of room. Don't we?" She looked at her parents.

"The sofa's quite comfortable," Milly's mother, Carole, said.

Sofa. Right. Was he surprised? Of course not. Had he expected them to offer him their daughter on a plate?

Cash rubbed the back of his neck. "That's mighty kind of you, but—"

"Maybe Cash has other friends in town," Carole said.

Hatchet Face nodded.

"Not exactly. But...I don't want to cause any bother."

"No bother," Milly said quickly.

"Of course not," her mother agreed. "We'd be delighted to have you."

Cash's gaze met Milly's father's. There was no delight evident on the old man's face. What there was was warning: *Keep your mitts off my daughter.*

Oh, yes. Cash swallowed. "Thank you. I appreciate that," he said to Milly and her mother.

Hatchet Face grunted and stabbed another piece of meat loaf.

She couldn't believe he'd come.
Cash Callahan. Here.
On her sofa!
It wasn't where she wanted him, of course. She wanted him right next to her in her bed—where she'd had him last time—where, if the truth were known, she'd had him in her heart every night since.

Of course no one else knew that but Milly, though she thought Alexis probably had guessed. Alexis had witnessed her distraction since Cash had left. She'd been forced to repeat things three and four times, had waved her fingers in front of Milly's face and said, "Hello-o-o? Anybody home?"

Finally she'd said, "Milly, give it up! Nobody is as lovesick as that after one night no matter how great it was!"

Milly never told her that nothing had happened. Alexis thought she was a mental case, anyway. If she'd found *that* out, Alexis would have her committed!

Anyway something *had* happened—she'd fallen in love.

Love? She could hear Alexis's mocking voice. Well, all right, maybe not love. She didn't know Cash well enough to love him. Yet.

But she was going to—she hugged herself with joy—because he'd come back!

He was asleep on the sofa at this very moment.

Now she eased open the door and peered in the darkness down the hallway toward the living room. A pair of socks protruded from the blanket that lay on the end of the sofa.

The sofa was too short for him.

"I can sleep there," she'd said an hour ago as they'd stood there comparing Cash's length to the sofa's and coming up long. "He can have my bed."

"He'll be fine," her father had said.

"But—"

"But nothing. I'm sure he's slept in more uncomfortable places. Haven't you?" Hatchet Face fixed Cash with a knowing look.

Cash nodded. "A few."

"And this is better than a park bench, right?" Milly's father hadn't even blinked.

"Right," Cash said.

"So," Milly's father said to her, "he'll be fine. Go to bed."

"I will. I...just want to say good night to Cash."

"Then say, 'Good night, Cash.'" He wasn't going to move until she did. She could tell.

Milly rolled her eyes. "Good night, Cash."

Cash grinned ruefully. "G'night, Milly."

"Sleep well," her father said to Cash. It sounded like an order to Milly.

Cash had seemed to think so, too. "Yes, sir."

So there he was—out in the living room on the sofa. And she was in the bedroom. Alone in her bed. And there was nothing she could do about it.

Except go out there now and see if he was all right.

Maybe he was getting a crick in his neck. Maybe he needed another blanket. And she didn't remember if she'd asked if he needed a toothbrush. Maybe he would want one, even if it was 2:42 in the morning.

And if he was perfectly fine?

Well, at least she could stand there for a few moments and watch him sleep.

She crept down the hall. In the moonlight she could make out Cash's still form beneath the blanket, but she couldn't see his features. She remembered when he had slept with her how his face had changed in sleep. The hard lines had softened. His dark lashes had made half moons against his cheekbones. His lips had parted slightly. She'd caught a glimpse of the boy he must have been. She wanted to see that same look again now.

She stepped closer, slipping across the rug on her bare feet soundlessly until she stood looking right down on him.

"You reckon it's me or you he's gonna shoot if he finds you out here?"

Milly jumped a foot. "Eee—!"

"Shh!" Cash swung himself to a sitting position and put a hand over her mouth. "For God's sake! You're gonna wake the dead, not just your old man!" He grabbed her hand, hauling her down onto the sofa next to him.

Milly's heart was pounding faster than a runaway stallion, and being pressed hard against Cash's body sure didn't slow it down. But she wasn't about to make any more noise. She moved her lips against his fingers to tell him so.

He yanked his hand away as if he'd been burned. "Cripes, Milly." A shudder ran through him. He made a fist, then wrapped his arm around her and hauled her close, kissing her hard. "You tryin' to drive me crazy?" he muttered against her lips.

"N-no," she murmured. But she felt dangerously close to insanity herself. He felt so good. Marvelous. Better even than she remembered. She melted against him, wrapped her arms around him.

"Feels like it," he whispered. His kiss deepened, his tongue touching hers, sending a shiver of longing straight through her. She'd never been kissed like that before! It was wonderful. *He* was wonderful.

Her father was going to kill him.

Ever since Dori had been seduced and abandoned, John Malone was convinced that if he'd been vigilant, it never would have happened.

His lapse with Dori—though it could hardly be called a

lapse, Milly thought; her sister had, after all, climbed out the bedroom window in the dead of night—was, John Malone was determined, never going to happen again.

Certainly not on the sofa in his very own living room!

Milly pushed herself away from Cash. "We can't!"

"But—"

"My father will kill us!"

"Be a great way to go." Cash's grin flashed in the darkness, and for a just a minute, Milly agreed. Then sanity reasserted itself—and with it, the desire for more than just one brief moment in Cash's arms.

They could have it all, she resolved, if they did things right.

"We can't," she said again, half sadly, half hopefully.

"Then why did you—" He broke off. She could almost feel the need vibrating from him. Even in the moonlight she could see the desire written in the taut expression on his face.

"I just...wanted to be with you. To remember...last time."

"You wanted *to remember* that?" He looked horrified.

She hugged her arms across her breasts. "It was all we had."

Cash snorted. "My fault."

"It was wonderful."

He just looked at her, then shook his head. "Right," he muttered. He fell back against the sofa and flung an arm across his eyes.

Tentatively she put a hand on his knee. He jerked and yanked his arm away to look at her again.

"I shouldn't've come. I just—" she broke off, unable to say why she had. "I'm sorry."

"'S all right. Not your fault." He pinched the bridge of his nose and shoved himself up straighter. "It's all right," he said again, and he managed a smile. "Things are just...conspirin' against us."

Milly mustered a smile, too. "We can't...you know," she said softly, ducking her head, unable to look at him.

"I know," he said.

They sat a moment in silence. Then she reached out and squeezed his hand. "I'm glad you came."

Cash's head was bent. He seemed to be staring down at their linked hands. Then his Adam's apple bobbed, and he let out a sort of shaky sound. "I guess I am, too," he said.

They sat there together for what seemed to Milly like hours, but could only have been a minute or two. She felt the warmth of Cash's hand curved around hers. She felt the heat of his thigh pressed against her leg. She felt her resolve begin to fade again, felt her heart begin to quicken and—

"I better go." She scrambled to her feet, then stopped, looking down at him. Their hands were still clasped. Impulsively she bent and brushed a quick kiss across his lips. "See you in the morning," she whispered, then turned and fled.

Behind her she heard Cash murmur, "Not if I see you first."

She was going to be the death of him.

Thanks to Milly Malone, he was going to die of terminal sexual frustration—or a gunshot wound thoughtfully provided by Hatchet Face.

The old man had clumped out to the kitchen twice during the night to get a glass of water and, incidentally, to make sure that Cash wasn't seducing his darling daughter on his living room sofa.

As if he would have, Cash's expression said indignantly, whenever Hatchet Face passed through.

Uh-huh.

It was providence, Cash reckoned, that Milly hadn't been

there when her father stomped through. If she had been, Cash would've been full of buckshot by now.

Instead he had a hell of a headache, gritty eyes, a crick in his neck and acute discomfort in a particularly sensitive area of his body. He wasn't sure the buckshot wouldn't have been preferable.

Until he saw Milly smiling across the breakfast table.

Suddenly he felt better. Stronger. Braver. Purer.

Pure? *Cash Callahan?*

He tested the notion. It was foreign, but not totally unwelcome. As a matter of fact, it didn't feel half-bad. He found himself smiling in return—even when Milly's father's eyes narrowed and gave him an assessing look.

Cash did his best to resemble innocence personified. He wasn't sure he was convincing.

John Malone turned his gaze on his daughter. "The whole day?" he asked, apparently questioning something she had been saying when Cash came into the kitchen.

"I don't have any classes," Milly said, buttering her toast. "And I worked nine hours on Saturday. Please, Dad?" The look she gave him was beseeching.

Ol' Hatchet Face hemmed and hawed, then finally grumbled, "I guess so. But don't make a habit of it."

"Oh, no, I won't!" Milly assured him. She beamed at Cash. "I've got the whole day off."

They went horseback riding.

Cash couldn't believe it. Talk about a busman's holiday! Pete and Rod would be howling if they knew he'd come all this way to sleep on a sofa and ride a stubborn swaybacked old sorrel.

But Milly had never been horseback riding before.

He gaped when she told him, but he knew better than to say, "Never?" because, after all, this was the same girl who'd never been to a rodeo.

"Do you mind?" she asked him, looking up at him with those eyes that made him turn to mush.

Mind? He didn't think he even had one anymore.

"Not at all," Cash said.

Milly thought she was dreaming.

If she was, she didn't want to wake up. Her father said she spent half her life thinking about things that never were and never would be. Maybe he was right. But this—*this!*— was better than any dream she'd ever had.

Cash was here. Smiling. Teasing. Tugging on her long dark braid. He made her laugh. He made her breathless. And once—just once—he rode up alongside her and stole a kiss.

It was so quick, she hardly believed he'd done it.

But then he winked at her and she knew it was a memory she would cherish for years.

The whole day was perfect. Like one of those wonderfully romantic novels she read and Dori rolled her eyes over because, as Dori said, "Things like that never happen in real life."

But right now—for just a few hours at least—they were happening to her!

The sun shone, but not too warmly. The breezes blew, but they were zephyrs, not a gale. The horse she rode was gentle.

"An old nag," Cash called it disgustedly, but Milly didn't care.

She didn't want a bronc. She just wanted to do something new, something different, something special, something that would always remind her of Cash.

In fact, she didn't think she would need any reminders of Cash. There was no way on earth she was going to forget him. He wasn't like any other guy she'd ever met.

She wasn't like any other girl he'd ever met.

She didn't giggle and she didn't simper, and if she laughed and smiled and tempted the hell out of him, it wasn't because she was trying to. She just seemed to enjoy what they were doing.

He couldn't believe she'd never been on a horse before; one glimpse of her in the saddle and he knew she was telling the truth. But she was eager, and she did what he told her, catching on quickly. And though they rode a long way up into the foothills quickly, and her legs and rear end must have been aching, she didn't complain. Not once.

She had packed them a picnic lunch, and they stopped on a rise overlooking the valley to eat. Cash got down first and went to catch her, knowing she'd wobble when she got off the horse.

She did, practically crumpling against him before she got her balance again. She clutched his arms and laughed shakily. "Sorry about that."

"No problem." Cash was enjoying holding her. "You all right? I reckon you'll be plenty sore tomorrow."

"Probably," Milly said. She pushed away gingerly. "But it's worth it."

"I could, um, give you a back rub?"

She laughed. "It isn't my back that hurts."

Cash grinned. "Ah, well. I could rub that, too."

"Thanks, but I think this is a little too public for that sort of thing."

Well, at least she didn't act shocked. At least she didn't say, "No way." Not that he'd expected her to. He knew a positive response when he felt one. Milly Malone had given him the most positive response he'd ever felt!

She tottered over and untied the rolled blanket she'd been carrying behind her saddle, then spread it out on the ground.

Cash helped get the food. His stomach growled.

Milly laughed. "I didn't realize I was starving you."

He grinned a little self-consciously. "Don't get many meals that smell this good."

She looked satisfied. "Well, help yourself."

They sat cross-legged on the blanket and ate potato salad and fried chicken that she'd made that morning, and Cash polished off the rest of last night's meat loaf as well.

Then Milly handed him a bag of cookies she'd also made that morning and Cash couldn't resist. He couldn't remember the last time he'd had homemade chocolate chip cookies. He must have downed a dozen before he lay back on the blanket and rubbed his belly. "Best meal I've had in years. Maybe ever."

"Good. Then you'll always remember."

"No fear of me forgettin' a meal like this."

"And the day?"

He turned his head to look at her when he heard the hesitancy in her words. Their gazes met, locked. And all the hunger that wasn't just for food, and all the need and all the frustration he'd been feeling since that morning when he'd had to leave her, wouldn't be denied. He reached out a hand and snagged hers.

She came to him willingly, even landing right on top of him when he tugged her that way. And when he touched his lips to hers, she kissed him with a longing that seemed to equal his.

It was wonderful. Marvelous. Better than all the chocolate chip cookies, fried chicken and potato salad in the world.

"Ah, yeah," Cash murmured, and rolled her beneath him.

"Ow."

He jerked, then pulled back to look down at her.

Milly gave him an apologetic smile. "S-sorry. I'm...just

a little sore. Stiff, you know," she added, "from the riding."

Of course she was. And he was an idiot. He scrambled off her.

"I'm okay," she said quickly.

But Cash knew better. "I owe you a back rub," he reminded her as he sat back on his heels and smiled at her.

She turned bright red. "I don't think—"

"C'mon," he said. He turned her around and got behind her and settled his hands on her back.

At first she was stiff under his touch. Rigid, almost. He pressed the pads of his thumbs against her spine and began to work his way down. A soft shudder coursed through her.

"Hurt?" he asked.

"Mmm? N-no." She flexed her shoulders. A sigh escaped her. "G-good," she said.

Cash smiled. He kept kneading, letting his hands move rhythmically over her back, then slide up to knead the taut cords of her neck.

Milly sighed and softened, her shoulders bent. She began to melt under his touch.

Cash's own body was about as far from melting as it could get. A fine tremor seemed to have settled in his fingers. He clenched his fists to stop it.

"Don't!"

"What?" He looked at her bent head, confused by her demand. "Don't what?"

"Don't stop."

He smothered a groan. No, God help him, he wouldn't stop. He cleared his throat. "Lie down," he commanded. His voice sounded ragged even to him.

For a long moment Milly didn't move. He thought she was going to argue. But then, wordlessly, she turned to lie on her stomach. Her T-shirt hiked up so he could see a couple of inches of her back. The same couple of inches he'd seen when she'd stood on tiptoe in her kitchen. But they were more accessible now.

He could touch them.

Cash took a careful breath, then straddled her thighs, settled lightly on them and let his fingers brush the bare skin above the waistband of her jeans.

Milly murmured softly. She didn't freeze up. On the contrary, she closed her eyes and pillowed her head on her hands and let him slide his fingers up her spine, beneath her shirt, against the warm, smooth skin of her back.

The breeze played with strands of her hair, blowing them over his hands. They felt like silk. *She* felt like silk everywhere he touched her.

It was better than he'd dreamed. He'd been thinking about touching Milly since the night he'd met her. He'd been dreaming about touching her since the morning after he'd fallen asleep.

And now...now he could touch her, stroke her, knead her smooth, supple flesh, bend his head and kiss the cotton that lay between his lips and her skin, ease the shirt up just a little higher, touch her spine with his mouth.

God, yes! His fingers trembled. It was all he could do to go slow, to force himself to take things easy.

She was young, he reminded himself. She was innocent. She might even be a virgin!

Cripes, it didn't bear thinking about! He might be *the first*.

It made him nervous as hell. He wanted it to be good for her—as good as he was sure it would be for him.

He wanted it to be *wonderful*.

He bent his head and touched his lips to the back of her neck.

"Wonderful," Milly murmured. "Marvelous."

"Yes." Only one word hissed out from between Cash's

lips. But it was pure agreement. She was right. It was the most wonderful feeling in the world.

His hands moved lower, caressing her backside. He knew it was sorer than her back so it had to need his touch even more.

The denim felt rough beneath his fingers—much rougher than Milly's skin. Colder than Milly's skin. More impersonal than Milly's skin. He wanted to touch Milly's skin.

His fingers curved beneath the denim, sliding down to caress the smooth skin of her buttocks and…

And she scrambled out from between his legs with such force that she knocked him backward onto his butt.

"What the—!" He gaped at her.

Milly rolled over and pulled her knees up to her chest, wrapping her arms around them, her eyes wide, her breath coming in gulps. "You know what," she said, still gulping air.

"I—"

"I don't want—" she stopped, the color high in her cheeks, and shook her head. "No, that's not true," she said after a moment. "I do want…I just…can't."

Cash scowled. "Can't?"

"Won't, I guess I should say."

As if *that* clarified a damn thing. "Won't?" His scowl deepened.

Milly bit her lip. "I have a sister," she said after a long silence. "And well…she did."

Cash was pretty sure that wasn't the end of the story, but he had a fair idea what the end of the story was. "Jake's mother?"

"Mmm." Milly picked at the edge of the blanket. "Dori's not like me. She's always really strong. Really determined. And sort of a rebel, too. She never listened much to anything Daddy said."

Having met Daddy, Cash had a fair amount of sympathy

for Milly's sister. "She rebelled against Daddy and had Jake?"

"Something like that," Milly said. "There was this guy who was in Livingston for a while. His name was Chris and he was a singer. A *good* singer. He was going places. And Dori…well, Dori loved him."

Cash ran his tongue over his lips and settled back, feeling the urgency slowly ebb. Not feeling the interest go away.

"He wasn't…Daddy's idea of a responsible guy. He didn't want Dori to have anything to do with him. He said Chris was unstable. Undependable. He said Chris was selfish and that when he wanted to move on, he would leave Dori without a backward glance."

"He said all that to your sister?" Cash shook his head in disbelief. How could a father be that dumb?

Milly nodded.

"And she didn't deck him?" Cash was outraged on Dori's behalf.

Milly smiled sadly. "Hardly. But she did what she thought was the next best thing. She ran away with Chris."

"Something tells me the story doesn't have a happy ending."

Milly shook her head. "Daddy was right. Chris wasn't dependable. Dori got pregnant and was sick, and he said he wasn't ready for that. He couldn't deal with it. He said he couldn't deal with her. Not then. When he grew up, maybe, he said. And he sent her home."

"She came?" Cash had trouble believing that, too.

But Milly said simply, "She was pregnant and jobless and she didn't have any money. Where else could she go?"

Nowhere. Cash understood. And the old man had been making her pay for it ever since. Cash sighed and settled back, propping himself on his hands. "And you're determined not to go the same route. Is that it?"

Milly flushed. "Raising a child alone isn't easy," she said, defending herself.

"I'm sure it isn't," Cash said. "But I wouldn't have got you pregnant!" He said the words a little gruffly, a little guiltily, because in fact, even protected, he knew he couldn't guarantee it.

"It isn't just that." Milly hugged her knees tightly. "It's important, of course. As little as Jake is, he misses having a dad. His friends have dads. He wants a dad. But—" she ducked her head again, and her voice dropped so he could barely hear her "—that's not the only reason I won't."

Cash wasn't sure he heard right. "Not the only…?"

Milly lifted her gaze, then, and met his. "I would like to make love with you," she said in a soft but firm voice, "but it would have to be 'making love.' When I make love, I want it to matter."

It matters! Cash wanted to say. To his deprived and aching body it mattered a whole hell of a lot! He'd been needing her for hours, for days, for *weeks!* Sometimes it felt liked he'd needed her forever.

But that wasn't what she meant.

And he knew what she meant—exactly what she said.

She meant she wanted to make love, not just to assuage desire or release or momentary satisfaction. What she wanted had nothing to do with the caress of silken skin, soft kisses or even desperate, hungry ones. It had to do with commitment and responsibility and vows.

God.

Cash didn't know the first thing about that kind of love! Not grown-up, responsible, give-and-take, committed adult love. He wasn't sure he *wanted* to know anything about it!

Not for a while yet. Not for years, actually. When he was forty…maybe then. Yeah, forty might be long enough.

But he didn't think Milly wanted to hear that.

He knew what Milly wanted to hear. And if he were a

real cad, he could say the words. He knew guys who would. They'd get what they wanted, and then they'd walk—just like Chris Whoever-He-Was had.

Or run. He supposed running was closer to the truth.

Well, maybe some guys could live with themselves if they did that.

Not Cash.

He rubbed the back of his neck. He scrubbed at his face with his hand. He reached out and snagged his hat from where it had fallen on the ground. Setting it on his head, he gave it a sharp tug, pulling it down.

"I'm sorry," Milly said in the face of his silence. "I shouldn't have brought you up here. I shouldn't have let you rub my...back. I shouldn't have—"

Maybe not. But Cash was honest enough to admit that the fault wasn't entirely hers.

"If you say you shouldn't have cooked me that fried chicken and made those cookies, I'm gonna say you're a flat-out liar," Cash said roughly. But he managed a grin that was rewarded when Milly stopped looking so stricken and relief flooded her face.

"You're not mad?"

Yes, he was. He was insane. He shook his head.

"You're—" her cheeks reddened "—all right?"

Cash shut his eyes for a brief moment, then shifted on the blanket, adjusting his jeans. "I reckon I'll live."

Milly scrambled to her feet and held out a hand to him.

Cash hesitated for just a second before he took it and let her haul him to his feet. Then damned if she didn't lean close and brush a kiss across his cheek. "Cash Callahan, I think you must be the sweetest man on the face of the earth."

Sweet, God help him!

Cash blinked, then blushed, then looked at the toes of his boots and shook his head despairingly. "Or the dumbest, I reckon."

Six

Dumb didn't even begin to describe him.

He needed his head examined. Not just for sleeping on the damn sofa or for going horseback riding or not doing what he really wanted to do with Milly Malone up there on the mountain, or even taking her back home after, smiling and untouched.

Those things were dumb, but they made a certain amount of scrupulous sense of the sort of which mothers were proud and, if they ever found out, gave you a pat on the head.

What made no sense at all—what was in fact the dumbest thing he ever did—happened two weeks after the horseback riding afternoon...two weeks after he kissed Milly Malone chastely on the lips and waved goodbye, determined to put her out of his mind for ever and ever. He came back!

For no good reason at all.

He *knew* he wasn't going to get anywhere—and still he came back.

This time, damned if she didn't talk him into going out in a canoe!

"A canoe?"

"I rode horses for you," she said as if that made it all right.

"I don't—I can't—" But when she looked at him that way, how the heck was he going to say no to her?

And that was how Cash Callahan, who couldn't swim a stroke, found himself in the middle of the Yellowstone River, paddling for all he was worth in a less-than-cooperative canoe.

He couldn't believe he was doing this. Couldn't imagine why he'd let her talk him into it. What was he going to get out of canoeing—besides wet?

And then he capsized—and suddenly he knew.

He was going down for the third time, regretting a misspent life and a complete lack of intimacies with Milly, when Milly threw her arms around him and hauled him to the bank.

The feel of her wet warm body pressed to his was enough to give him heart failure.

But then she crouched over him, big eyes pleading. "Are you all right? Tell me you're all right. Do you need artificial resuscitation?"

And Cash swallowed the last of the river and gasped, "Yes, please!"

She laughed. She sat back on her heels and actually laughed at him! And then she bent down, pressed her breasts against his chest and touched her lips to his. Cash understood why they called it the "kiss of life." But when she was finished, his heart was beating so fast he thought he needed resuscitation more after her kiss than before!

He should have quit while he was ahead.

He wasn't going to get to sleep with her—and hanging around with Milly was dangerous to his mental health.

Except he had such a damn good time with her, he tended to forget how frustrated he felt the minute he was leaving again.

That had to be why, three weeks later, when he and Pete and Rod were on their way to Billings, Cash found himself stopping to see her once more.

"Billings isn't far," Milly said. "Do you mind if I come with you? Then you could come back here after. Spend a day or two," she said hopefully. "If you want to."

Pete and Rod grinned at each other. "Oh, we'd love that," Rod said.

Cash glowered at them. "She isn't ridin' with you idiots." The last thing he needed was them making sly comments in front of Milly. "Can we take your car?"

Milly beamed at him. "Of course."

"Ho boy, you better watch yourself," Rod said when Milly went back inside and Cash was getting his rigging bag out of the back. "She's gonna have you roped an' tied before Christmas."

"Don't be a jerk," Cash growled. "She's a friend. That's all."

"Some friend," Pete whistled. "Wish I had me one like her."

Cash poked a finger in his face. "Don't even think it, buster."

Pete pulled his head back. He glanced at Rod, then gave Cash a quick nervous smile. "No fear."

Cash went with Milly to the rodeo in Billings. He rode well, placed in the money and felt even better about it because she was there cheering him on. "You're my lucky girl," he told her after, looping an arm over her shoulders.

Milly wrapped her arm around his waist. "I hope so."

He spent the first half of the week with her—and her

parents. Milly was helping her dad build a garage, and Cash offered to help. He was good with a hammer and nails. Besides, he got to put his arms around her while they were putting up wall braces, and he got to feel her jean-clad rear end brush against him while she laughed and talked, and her old man didn't even seem to notice.

Cash felt smug—as if he was getting away with something. Trouble was, he wasn't getting away with what he wanted. These days with Milly were part heaven—and part hell.

Milly thought it was heaven. She said so.

She said he was marvelous, and even the old man grudgingly agreed that Cash could be useful now and again. "When he isn't ogling you," Milly's father said to her.

"Cash doesn't ogle, Dad," Milly said, then favored him with such a particularly wonderful smile that Cash, ogling, whacked his thumb with the hammer.

"Sheeee—!"

"Aw, Cash. Poor baby," she crooned, hurrying over to take his hand in hers. "Let me."

She kissed it and made it better.

Or if it wasn't better—at least it was distracted. Now he ached somewhere else.

"What the hell happened to you?" Pete asked when they picked him up on their way to San Francisco.

Cash mumbled something about a hammer. Pete and Rod exchanged knowing looks.

"She's gonna get you," Pete said again.

"No, she ain't." The season was coming to a close. After the finals he would take a few weeks off, go see his folks in Texas—he guessed they were still in Texas— maybe do a little fishing with his brothers Mac and Joe. Forget all about Milly Malone.

Trouble was, he had a stake in her old man's garage now. He had to stop and see how it was. The whole west wall was his doing. It wouldn't be there—not as sturdy, not as straight—if it hadn't been for him.

And Milly—well, Milly wasn't so easy to forget, after all.

He missed her when he didn't see her every few weeks. He looked forward to her smiling face, her eager greeting. He even welcomed the chance to help her wallpaper the dining room for her mother. Paste fights were pretty interesting—as long as you got into them when no one else was home.

He thought about the garage and the dining room—and Milly—pretty often. Sometimes he got lonely enough that he actually called her on the phone.

She was always thrilled to hear from him. She wanted to hear all about where he was, what horses he had ridden, what he was planning to do. He liked telling her. It made things sort of...well, more meaningful...having somebody to share them with.

She was the one he called every time he won. His "good luck girl."

Rod and Pete kept their mouths shut about his phone calls. They watched, and maybe between themselves they speculated. But they never said much to Cash.

Only once as he stopped to pick Cash up after a three-day visit with Milly the next spring, did Rod ask, "You're really gettin' serious, aren'tcha?"

Cash said no. "She's my friend, that's all." He was watching her in the rearview as Rod pulled away. He could see her waving, waving, waving...until the truck was out of sight.

"Friend?" Rod echoed quietly.

Cash shrugged. "Aw, well, you know."

Rod slanted him a glance. "No, I don't know."

Cash stared at the window, watched his reflection in the

glass. He ran his tongue over his lips, lips that still tasted Milly Malone. "I don't, either," he mumbled.

And that was the long and short of it, right there.

There had never been another girl like Milly in his life. And there didn't seem to be words to describe how he felt about her. God knew he still wanted her—and had still never even had her—but sometimes he actually forgot about that.

Sometimes he was so taken with just talking to her or listening to her or going hiking or horseback riding or, heaven help him, canoeing with her, that he didn't dwell on those long lonely nights on the sofa in her parents' house.

He learned to live with them.

And still—someday, he promised himself—he hoped.

But *serious?*

He wasn't really *serious* about her, was he?

Hell, he was a kid. He'd just turned twenty-five a couple of months ago. Well, make that eight months ago. But twenty-five wasn't old. Not old enough to be serious about anybody at least.

Sure, some of his buddies were getting married. Some of them were even fathers. Some were going on two. Frankly, the whole idea scared Cash to death.

He liked reading to Jake, who was better about sitting still and listening this year. He liked giving the little boy horsey rides and playing hide-and-go-seek with him. But he damned sure wasn't ready to put a little critter of his own to bed every night and get up with him in the morning.

He'd take a lot of lonely nights on the sofa to prevent that!

He told Milly as much.

"I ain't ready for this sort of thing," he said whenever they baby-sat her nephew. "Or *that* sort of thing," he said once, when he found her leafing through the new bride magazines when she shelved them at her dad's store.

"I know," she always said promptly and turned to him with a smile and a hug. "I'm not, either. I've got college to finish."

"An' I gotta win the world."

Cash had made it to the NFR the last three years in a row. He'd finished fourteenth the first year, seventh the second and fifth last year. He was getting closer. And hadn't his daddy always said, "Fourth time's a charm"?

Surely he'd win it this year.

But when December rolled around, and he went to Vegas again, he couldn't find the rhythm. Not the winner's rhythm. He finished sixth.

"Sixth!" he told Milly angrily on the phone afterward.

"I know," she said soothingly. "I know."

She didn't know. Nobody knew, damn it. Not unless they'd been there themselves.

"Can I help?" she asked him softly.

Cash wished she was there to put her arms around him. Sometimes a fellow needed a friend. He dragged in a deep breath. "Naw. I'm just bummed. I'll be all right in a couple weeks." He forced a grin. "Right and ready to go again."

"Of course you will," Milly said. "Of course you will."

He went to Texas after the finals. He helped his old man build a fence. It reminded him of Milly's dad's garage. He helped his mother wallpaper the bathroom.

"Where did you get to be so domestic?" she asked him.

"Oh, I helped a friend once," he said vaguely.

His mother raised her brows. His brothers exchanged looks.

"So are we goin' fishin' or not?" he asked them.

They spent a week in Oklahoma, caught their limit of large-mouth bass and a passel of catfish. They cooked them outdoors over the campfire and Joe said it was the best outdoor meal he'd ever had.

Cash remembered Milly's fried chicken and thought the fish came second. He wondered if she'd like to try her hand at fishing the next time he got up that way. They'd never gone fishing. He started making plans.

"Cash?" she yelped, throwing herself at him when he turned up on her doorstep at the end of March. Then, "Fishing?" she said when he broached the subject. There was still a foot of snow on the ground. "Ice fishing?"

"What's the matter?" he teased. "Chicken? Too old for a little fun?"

"I am not," Milly said stoutly. "I'll come."

That was the year they did a lot of fishing. Every time he came through Livingston, he took her out to one of the nearby rivers. She always came with him. She never complained.

Cash was the one who was complaining. He couldn't seem to get farther up the standings than tenth. He worried about it, fumed about it, talked about it. How was he going to win the world if he didn't have a good slot going in?

"Any one of the top fifteen riders could win," Milly pointed out again and again. "You've told me that yourself."

"Yeah." But it was easier to believe if you were sitting fifth or sixth—or better yet, second or third.

Last year he'd been further out than before. And he wasn't getting any younger. He was twenty-seven now. This year he'd better finish higher. Maybe, he told himself, last year was the dip before the win.

"I'm gonna do it," he told Milly.

"I gotta do it," he told himself.

But when December rolled around, it turned out not to be the dip before the win. It turned out to be the dip before an even bigger dip. He dropped from tenth to twelfth.

He began to get scared, remembering something his mother used to say: something about being always a bridesmaid and never a bride.

Or maybe that was Milly.

It wasn't bad enough he was crashing in the standings, but when he came back to Montana for his first visit of the spring, his best friend seemed only to have weddings on the brain!

Every time he wanted to talk about broncs, Milly wanted to talk about bridal gowns. Every time he brought up the standings, she told him who just got engaged.

Her friend Alexis, no candidate for forever as far as Cash could see, was tying the knot the first part of May. Milly was going to be maid of honor.

"In blue jeans, believe it or not," she giggled.

A high school friend, whose name was Gina or Tina or Lena or something, was getting married three weeks later. "Formal," Milly said.

Even Pete was getting hitched to a little barrel racer he'd met in Laramie last summer. They were getting married in the local rodeo arena, Milly told him.

She wanted to drag him to them all.

"Can't," Cash said flatly. "They get married on Tuesday night, I can be there. Weekends are out. You know that. I gotta ride."

"You could take one weekend off," Milly said. They were sitting side by side on the bank of Brackett Creek. They hadn't caught a thing.

"I am takin' a weekend off. I'm comin' to see you graduate, aren't I?" Cash slanted a grin her way. That was what she ought to be thinking about—not getting married, for heaven's sake.

And not just because she was finally going to have her degree, which was great in itself, but because she had a job lined up in Denver once she did.

Denver.

Milly was moving to Denver. In a matter of weeks.

She was going to be an accountant. An accountant with an apartment. An apartment with a bed.

Cash was determined that there was going to be a bed.

She loved him.

Had loved him for three years. Probably she'd fallen a little bit in love with him that very first night she'd slept with him—even if *slept* had been the operative word.

For sure she'd fallen deeply, madly, totally in love with Cash Callahan as time went on—and she stayed where she was.

And Cash kept coming back.

She'd never thought he would.

She'd been amazed that first time he'd turned up in the grocery store. She'd been almost as surprised and as gratified the second time, a few weeks later, when he'd appeared on her parents' front porch.

After that, even though Milly had told herself she wasn't counting on him, she knew she was.

Cash was the bright spot in her life. The little bit of "fast-lane glitz" in her otherwise humdrum existence.

He brought fun and laughter and excitement, deep powerful kisses and long warm hugs into her life. He brought 1:00 a.m. phone calls from places she'd never heard of, and stuffed alligators from Florida when he missed her birthday because he was riding in Kissimmee and tales of cowboy high jinks here and there and everywhere that made her laugh until she thought she'd wet her pants.

Knowing that Cash was "out there" and would again sometime be "right here" made the boring sameness of her days bearable. He made her stuffy professors tolerable, her father's petty irritations endurable. He gave her hope and laughter and the courage to look beyond them all.

She loved him.

And when she graduated...

As soon as she graduated...

Once she graduated...

She would have a life of her own.

And she would have Cash.

Having Cash made the promise of graduation mean more than she ever thought it would. He gave her the courage to move out, to determine to say goodbye to Livingston, to face the big wide world.

It was Cash who had got her a subscription to the *Denver Post*. It was Cash who'd sent her giveaways from the Denver Chamber of Commerce every time he passed through. It was Cash who found accountancy firms for her to apply to, banks that could use her services, CPAs who were advertising for help.

"You're a regular one-man placement service," she told him.

He glanced up from where he was circling want ads in the paper and muttered something about having "a vested interest."

Milly raised her brows. "What?"

"Never mind."

But she couldn't help thinking about it...dreaming about it. A *vested interest?* Did he mean what she hoped he meant?

Did he mean *marriage?*

Milly, even though she told herself not to, dared to hope. Especially when he told her, laughing, that he wasn't about to do this job hunting for anyone else. "I'm only doing this for us."

Us.

It was the most beautiful word in the English language. Next to *Cash,* of course.

* * *

Cash was counting the days.

Milly had a job in Denver. The last time he'd driven through, he'd found her an apartment. Furnished. With a bed.

Just what the cowboy ordered.

He spent a lot of long nights going down the road thinking about it. About her.

"You oughta just marry her," Pete had said a few months back. He was going to quit rodeoing after his wedding. "She's prettier than you two," was the way Pete had put it at first. Then he'd sobered and said, "Naw, it's time. That's all. Time to grow up."

"No," Cash said. He wasn't ready for that.

Rod was slowing down, though, too. He'd broken his leg bad at Calgary last year and had had a hard time coming back. He'd planned to jump in with both feet, but it wasn't happening. Cash wasn't surprised when Rod told him he'd better start looking for somebody else.

"You're givin' up?" Cash couldn't believe it.

"Gettin' realistic," Rod said.

"Well, fine. Suit yourself." Cash would go on alone. Or with a couple of other guys. It wasn't hard to find cowboys to chase the rainbow with. There was no shortage of dreamers on the rodeo circuit.

Cash remembered Shane Nichols. He hadn't won the world, either, and he wanted it just as bad.

When he asked Shane if he'd like a traveling partner, Shane had been pleased. "I'll take the bull riding. You take the broncs. We'll knock 'em dead."

And sure enough, they seemed to be doing it.

By the week of Milly's graduation both of them were in the top five, only a couple of thousand dollars off the leader. The horses were good 'uns. The rhythm was there. Every body part Cash had was in prime working order.

One part, of course, damned well ought to be—as rested as it was!

But that, he promised himself, was going to change.

As soon as Milly moved to Denver.

There were twenty days left; he had just jumped four places in the standings; and he was close to the top of the world when he called her that Sunday from a pay phone in Tulsa.

"Milly? Hey, babe, how ya doin'?" He was grinning from ear to ear, eager to share the news.

"Oh, Cash, thank God!"

"What's wrong?"

"My father's had a heart attack."

She knew he'd come.

Of course he'd come. He was her best friend in all the world. More than that—he was the man she loved.

And she was sure Cash loved her.

He may not have come right out and said so, but she knew Cash wasn't the sort of guy to wear his heart on his sleeve. He showed his love, so he didn't have to say it.

"Don't count on it," Dori said darkly.

The look on her mother's face said much the same. If even a solid, responsible man like John Malone could have a heart attack and be barely hanging on to life by a thread, how could you trust any man?

"He'll come," Milly said firmly to them both. "I need him to," she added in a whisper only she could hear.

He came. He was coming up the steps to the hospital Tuesday morning as Milly was coming down them. She didn't even see him at first. She wasn't seeing much, not having slept in almost three days.

She actually felt him first, before she saw him. Strong familiar arms came around her when she stumbled, trying to sidestep whoever was in her way, and she started, then looked up to see Cash's beloved face searching hers.

"God, Mil, you look like hell."

A smile flickered on her lips. It was the first smile she'd managed since her father had collapsed Saturday afternoon. It made her face feel as if it were cracking. "Ah, Cash, you always were a flatterer." She blinked back tears.

He turned her and wrapped an arm around her shoulder, hugging her close as they walked back up the hospital steps. "I saw your mother. I know how your dad is. How are *you?*"

She told him. After they went to see her father, they stopped for a cup of coffee, then they went down and walked by the river. He still held her hand, and that was the most important thing. There wasn't much to say. She didn't want to talk, anyway. She just wanted him to hold her.

She didn't tell him that, either, though, but he seemed to understand. He took her gently in his arms and kissed her cheek. Then they simply stood there, locked together, supporting each other.

That was the wonderful thing about Cash. He understood.

And she knew he'd understand when she told him what else she'd decided.

"Cash?"

"Mmm?" His lips were in her hair.

"I can't go to Denver."

Seven

It was the right thing to do.

It was the only thing she *could* do.

Milly knew that. She'd known it since the moment it happened. At first she'd hoped for a miracle: that her father would bounce back and be his old self in a matter of days, that he'd come home and be able to plunge right back into the insanity of working fourteen hour days seven days a week.

But of course he didn't.

If there was a miracle, it was that John Malone had lived at all.

He had. But the road back was going to be long and hard. And if there was going to be anything to come back to, it would be up to Milly to preserve it.

Dori was willing to help, which actually surprised Milly a little. Dori and her father had not been on good terms for years. It had only partly to do with the wandering Chris and the out-of-wedlock child. The real rift had begun years before when John Malone had thrown his only son, Deke, out of the house.

Dori had taken her brother's part—and afterward she'd been even more rebellious than her brother. The difference was that she was his daughter. John Malone had different standards for girls.

His standards didn't include sleeping with unreliable men and having their children, however. Milly had always thought that part of the reason Dori had taken up with Chris was that he was so "unsuitable." If it was the reason she'd got pregnant, Milly had never asked. Still, she wouldn't have been surprised.

The surprise was that, once Jake was born, John Malone seemed to dote on this child whose very existence he had rued from the day he'd known of it.

Maybe that was why Dori was so willing to do what she could. When Milly asked, Dori said simply, "He needs it. What else would I do?"

And then Milly did understand. When Dori had needed him, even when—*especially when*—she hadn't wanted to, John Malone had come through. He'd always been there for them when they needed him, supporting, striving, bolstering.

Save Deke, of course. Milly couldn't help but feel sad about the unresolved bitterness between her father and brother. But that wasn't something she could do anything about.

This she could. And did.

It was a good thing, too. When he came home from the hospital three weeks later, John Malone could barely walk from the bedroom to the living room. He couldn't get to the kitchen without pausing to rest. He couldn't go down to the basement at all.

It was all too clear that he wasn't going to be opening

the store on Monday—or on any day in the foreseeable future.

No, if Milly hadn't realized it before, she did now—her commitment to the Malone grocery store was going to be for the long haul.

There would be no going to Denver in the foreseeable future. No new job. No wonderful apartment.

And Cash?

Of course there would be Cash, she assured herself.

He loved her. He had been there for her for three years. He was disappointed about Denver, of course. They both were. But he understood. She was sure he did.

He'd gone quite still, wooden almost, when she'd told him. He'd almost seemed to stop breathing. Startled, Milly had stepped back in his embrace to look up at him. He was staring down at her, a stunned expression on his face.

"You know I have to stay," she'd said earnestly. Her fingers tightened against his back. "Don't you?"

He seemed to be gathering himself together. Then, at last, he nodded. "I know." His voice was colorless, flat. Distant, almost.

"It isn't that I wouldn't *like* to go to Denver," she went on, worried now.

"I know," he said again. But already he seemed more remote, as if he was pulling away even though he didn't move.

Milly knew how much Cash had been looking forward to her move—even more than she had. She remembered again his words, "I'm doing this for us." It was a thought she'd hugged to herself for months.

There would still be an "us," she wanted to tell him. But she couldn't tell him when. She knew there was a limit to Cash's patience. She tried not to believe that this was it.

"Denver will still be there," she'd said a little desperately.

"Sure."

"And I'll have a lot more experience when I go."

"Right."

"It isn't forever, Cash."

"No." He'd smiled at her then, but for the first time his smile didn't reach his eyes.

And though he gave her a thumbs-up and a bone-crushing Cash Callahan hug when he left later that afternoon, for the first time in three years, she wondered if she would ever see him again.

She wasn't going to Denver!

He couldn't believe it. He'd been counting the weeks, the days—hell, he'd practically been counting the *hours*—and now she wasn't going to go. She was going to stay in Livingston, work at the blasted grocery store, waste her whole damn life.

It wasn't fair to think that. Cash *knew* it wasn't fair to think that. He knew her father needed her, and that Milly was only doing what she believed she had to do. But it still annoyed the hell out of him.

He'd been counting on her!

Then he realized with a jolt that he had no right to.

Milly wasn't his.

He turned that over in his mind. The awareness came as something of a shock. Over the past three years, he'd grown used to counting on her. He'd sure as hell been counting on Denver!

Milly had heard that saying about life being what happened to you while you were making other plans. She'd always thought it wasn't such a bad idea. Life had always seemed more exciting than her plans.

Not lately. Lately Milly's life had been reduced to tin cans, cardboard boxes, purchase orders, ledger sheets and frequent, reassuring phone calls to her father to convince him that no, the grocery store hadn't gone under.

Yet.

There was always a *yet* as far as John Malone was concerned. No one, he was fond of saying, worked as hard as he had. No one could do the job that he had done for forty years. No one could live up to his standards. No one could get it quite right.

But, damn it all, Milly tried.

She shouldn't have been surprised. Her father had always been a hard taskmaster. For as long as she could remember, he'd demanded perfection—his notion of perfection. He set standards that left little room for breathing, let alone errors.

She wanted to say, "You think you could do better? Get in here and do it yourself!"

But of course, she didn't. He wasn't well enough to come back. Wasn't that why she was here, after all? He was her father. She loved him. And she knew how much the store meant to him. He'd given his life to it.

The least she could do was give it a few months.

Or years, a dismayed little voice said deep inside her head.

Milly tried not to think about that.

It wouldn't be *years,* she assured herself. She wouldn't be stuck here forever. Someday she would be free again to live her own life, have her own hopes, follow her own dreams.

Someday.

But no time soon, that was for sure.

It was all Milly's fault.

Cash broke his leg in Las Vegas, and it was all Milly's fault.

If she'd moved to Denver the way she was supposed to,

he wouldn't have even been in Vegas competing. He'd have been helping her move.

But she hadn't gone to Denver. She'd stayed home to mind the store. And he'd thought, fine, if that's the way she's going to be about it, he could find a lucrative way to spend the weekend.

"I thought you'd come here, anyway," she'd said when he'd called to tell her his change of plans.

"Can't," he'd replied rather more abruptly than was necessary. "I'd have helped you move, but since you're not going to…well, I'm in fifth place now. If I win in Vegas I'll be sitting good goin' into summer."

"If that's what you want," Milly had said quietly.

It wasn't what he wanted. He wanted her to move to Denver, damn it! But he wasn't getting that. So she wasn't getting him to go to Livingston and spend the night on the couch!

"I'll see you later in the summer."

"Right." He thought she sounded a little sad. Good. Maybe she'd miss him—maybe she'd miss what they could have had if she'd gone to Denver!

"Well," she added, "good luck."

She probably should have said, "Break a leg." That was what they said before people went on stage to wish people luck, wasn't it? A sort of reverse psychology.

But she hadn't. She'd said, "Good luck," and here he was sitting in the damned emergency room with a broken leg and a doctor saying, "I wouldn't plan on riding again before the first of August. How'd you say you did it?"

Cash explained. It had been a freak accident. The horse he'd drawn had spooked in the chute, smashing him back. His spur caught between the rail and the standard. When the horse jerked up again, the spur stayed where it was. His leg snapped.

"Couldn't happen again in a million years," the doctor

told him cheerfully. "You were in the wrong place at the wrong time, that's all. You should have been somewhere else."

No kidding, Cash thought. He tipped his head back and shut his eyes, in the blackness seeing his entire season go down the drain.

The doc was right. He should damned well have been in Denver!

He didn't tell Milly.

His mama had always said, "If you can't say something nice, don't say nothin' at all."

Cash figured the chances of him saying something not very nice were pretty high. He didn't blame her exactly...well, yes, he did...exactly. But it wasn't nice of him to do so. It wasn't even right of him to do so. He knew it. He couldn't help it.

A part of him wanted to call and rail at her. A part of him wanted to call and say, "I'm hurt. I'm comin' home."

But the rational part knew better. He couldn't call and rail at her because it wasn't really her fault no matter what he thought. And he couldn't call and say, "I'm hurt. Take care of me," because she had enough to take care of at the moment.

Milly had her father. She had his store. She had more commitments and responsibilities than she could handle right now. She wouldn't need him, too.

So when the doc let him out, he caught a ride to Texas. Home, after all, was where, if you went there, they had to take you in.

She thought he'd come.

At least she thought he'd call to talk, to tell her how things were going, to see how she was doing here. She knew he'd been upset that she couldn't leave her family, but she was sure he'd get over it before too long.

But days turned into weeks, and the weeks became a month and then two. The Livingston Fourth of July rodeo came and went, so did the Wilsall and the Wolf Point and even Glasgow, which he usually fit in between runs down to Cheyenne. But the entire months of June and July came and went and Cash Callahan never came to call.

Which meant what? she asked herself.

That he had given up on her? That they were no longer friends? That he no longer cared?

She didn't want to believe it. But she didn't know what else to think.

"Where's Cash?" her nephew, Jake, asked her at least a dozen times over the summer. Jake was five now and fixated on cowboys. Whenever Cash came, Jake followed him everywhere. "Do you think he's like my dad?" he'd ask her.

"The best parts of him," Milly always said. She hadn't really known Chris, but she was feeling more charitable toward him at the moment than toward Cash.

"Wish he'd come again," Jake said mournfully.

Milly knew how he felt.

She could have paged him. She had his pager number. But she didn't want to do it—not after the way they'd left things. If he didn't want her anymore, she didn't want to go chasing him. If he came back, well…then she would know.

"Either way, you'll know," Dori reminded her.

Yes, but ever the optimist—albeit a fading one at the moment—Milly didn't want to think about that.

She thought, instead, about how she was going to cope with her father. Never the easiest man to get along with, John Malone hated the inactivity his heart attack had forced on him. He didn't believe that anyone could do anything as well as he did it—and as long as he'd had plenty to do himself, he was only a minor irritant in Milly's life.

But once he sat idle all day and thought about how *Milly* ought to do things—how *he'd* do them if only he could— well, it didn't take long until she was ready to scream. She discovered very quickly that she couldn't work for him full-time and live with him, too.

She didn't want to talk about shelving string beans over a nine-o'clock dinner after she'd spent fourteen hours at the store. She didn't want to think about string beans at all. She didn't want to know what *he* would have said to get the tortilla chip people to stop giving them bags that looked more like they held corn flakes than corn chips. She didn't want to think about tortilla chips, either.

She didn't have a life anymore. She'd accepted that.

But she did need some space. In August she found an apartment over an outfitter's shop downtown and announced she was moving out.

"Are you sure, dear?" her mother said. "I mean, you don't have time to cook as it is."

"I'll buy microwave dinners." It would be a small price to pay.

It was a very small price indeed. Her father came back to work for a couple of hours every afternoon that month. He had more ideas. More directions. More suggestions. More criticisms. Bossing. Grumbling. Do this. Do that. Do it faster. Stack it straighter. Do it my way.

Milly bit her tongue and did what he said, then went home and determinedly forgot him and the store.

Her mother called her nightly on the telephone. "Aren't you lonely?" she asked.

"No," Milly had replied. "I'm not."

But she was.

For Cash.

It had been months and there had been no word. That said it all, just as Dori had told her it would.

"You need a life," Dori told her. "You work too hard."

"There's the pot calling the kettle black," Milly retorted.

"I have Jake."

Milly nodded. Sometimes she envied Dori for having Jake. He was a warm, cheerful presence to come home to at night. He was an endless supply of questions, a never-ending demand for cowboy stories, a perennially inquisitive little person who took his mother's mind off her troubles. And he was also the sign of a once-upon-a-time connection between Dori and a man she'd loved.

It was for that Milly envied Dori most.

As she shelved her macaroni and stacked her brussels sprouts and fought with the computer that didn't want to enter the shipment of eggs, she could think she was getting by, that she was doing okay. Not great, maybe…but at least all right. But at night when she went back to her little apartment over the outfitter's shop and curled up in her solitary bed, she remembered never having had that connection with Cash.

She wondered over and over what would have happened if he'd stayed awake longer that night, if instead of falling asleep in her arms, he'd fallen asleep in her body—after they'd made love.

What would it have been like to make love with Cash Callahan?

She'd said she never wanted "just sex," that she'd always wanted to "make love." She'd believed that then. Maybe she still believed it now. But the nights were long— and her arms and heart were lonely.

She dreamed about Cash. She dreamed about loving him.

Dreams were all she had now.

"Well, aren't you a sight for sore eyes." Carole Malone beamed when she opened the door and found Cash on the porch. "Milly and John are still at the store, but they'll be home in a few minutes. Did you go there first? No, of course you didn't, or you'd be with Milly. Come in. Sit down. Have a beer?"

Cash came in. He wasn't exactly sure of his welcome. He hadn't been to see them since John had had his heart attack. At first he'd been disgruntled and aware of how selfish that was. Then he'd broken his leg. By the time he was up and hobbling, he couldn't afford to go to see them—and it had been so long he wasn't sure what to say.

He could have called, of course. But he didn't know how Milly would react. There was always the chance that she would hang up on him. He thought it would be a damn sight harder for her to bodily throw him out of the house.

He sipped the beer while Carole made coleslaw and talked. "It's been so long. Milly will be delighted. Did you tell her you were coming?"

Cash shook his head. "We haven't…talked. Is John…?"

"He's doing much better." Carole shot him a quick smile and kept chopping cabbage. "He goes in to work a couple of hours each day. It isn't much, but it's a start. I don't know what we'd have done without Milly." She glanced out the window. "Oh! Here they come now. On time for once."

Cash stood up as the back door opened and Milly came in.

She was carrying a bag of groceries. Her cheeks were flushed from the wind, her long dark hair was tangled. He thought he remembered how pretty she was, but his memories hadn't even come close. Just looking at her, he felt his heart seem to catch in his throat.

He didn't speak, but he must have made a sound because at that very moment she saw him.

"Cash!" Milly blinked, her jaw dropped, then she flung the grocery bag on the table and flung herself into his arms.

He caught her, hauling her close, hugging her hard, then kissing her—right there in front of her mother and ol' Shotgun John Malone—because he couldn't help himself. It had been so long—*too* long!

A loud throat clearing sounded behind her, and Cash looked up to see John Malone in the doorway. He looked as if he'd aged ten years—but even that was better than the last time Cash had seen him.

"See how much better he is," Milly said eagerly to Cash.

Cash saw. He smiled. "Lookin' good," he said.

John made a harrumphing sound and went to get himself a beer. "Sit down," he commanded Cash.

"What's wrong with your leg?" Milly demanded when Cash moved to do just that.

Trust Milly to notice right off the bat. "Broke it," Cash said.

Milly's eyes got wide. "What? When?"

"In Vegas. Last week in May." He had to say that much. He didn't know whether she'd make the connection or not.

The look on her face told him that she had. "Oh, Cash!" She looked stricken.

"I'm all right," he said. "Now."

But she knew about rodeo. She knew that when he was hurt bad enough not to ride, he didn't make any money. "The standings?" she whispered.

Cash shook his head. "You don't want to know."

"Oh, Cash!" She hugged him. "Are you all right now?"

"Gettin' better. Gettin' back to it. Not full strength yet, but I'm tryin'. I've only been goin' down the road the last couple of weeks. I was in Texas before that."

"I thought—" Milly broke off. She shook her head.

"Never mind. Is dinner about ready?" she asked her mother. "I'm starved."

Cash didn't press her. He didn't have to. He knew what she was going to say—that she'd thought he hadn't come because he was mad, because he was through with her.

If he had the sense God gave a mule, he would be. One look at Milly and he was wanting her again the way he always did when he was around her. One evening with her and he'd be back in it up to his ears. And as sure as God had given ol' John a shotgun, Cash would be on the couch by himself.

No. He wasn't going to do that.

He'd call Pete or see if maybe Shane was up at his brother's. He'd find himself somewhere else to stay for the night.

It was bad enough that he couldn't keep his eyes off her, that his hands wanted to creep beneath the table to touch hers. His body almost leaned in her direction every time he so much as glanced her way.

When their elbows brushed while they were sitting side by side at the table, Cash felt as if an electric shock had gone right through him. When her breast brushed against his arm when she was clearing the table, the lightest touch jolted him where he sat.

"Huh?" he said to John, who was in the middle of pontificating about the state of the Montana economy and its effect on small businesses.

John frowned. "Got ears, boy? Pay attention now."

Cash did his best. They ate Carole's best apple cake with mugs of strong coffee after the meal, and just as Cash was thinking maybe he'd make a getaway, Dori showed up with Jake.

"Cash!" The little boy was thrilled. "You're back."

He couldn't leave right then. He had to talk to Dori, who watched him narrow-eyed and assessing. He had to wrestle with Jake, who squirmed and wriggled and whooped and hollered and said, "We gonna do this again tomorrow?"

"I gotta be gettin' on," Cash said, glancing at his watch. He gave Milly an apologetic look.

"Me, too," she said.

He blinked. "You? Going where?"

"Home. My apartment," she explained. There was a small smile just touching the corners of her mouth.

Cash's heart lurched. He scrambled up off the floor, still holding Jake, and set the little boy on his feet.

"Apartment?" Cash almost couldn't get the word out.

"Yes," Milly said. "Downtown. A one-bedroom over the outfitter's shop." She paused. "Would you like to see it?"

Cash swallowed audibly. His mouth was suddenly dry, his palms suddenly damp. "Milly?" he said hoarsely.

"Would you?"

"I would," he said.

Oh, yes.

Eight

He should have behaved himself.

Not a chance.

He'd wanted Milly forever. He'd kept his hands off her for years! He wasn't going to keep his hands off her tonight. Not unless she made him.

She didn't make him.

She drove her car in front of him, leading the way to her apartment. Cash followed, not sure whether to believe this was really happening.

He'd anticipated Denver for so long. He'd waited for Milly so long. And he'd had his hopes well and truly squashed. He'd been angry, then distant, then determined to put her out of his mind.

Yeah, right. Uh-huh.

Well, he'd tried.

Maybe God was rewarding him for good behavior. *Uh-huh, again.* Somehow he didn't think God was doing anything—except maybe setting him up for a fall.

"So don't get your hopes up," he cautioned himself as he pulled into the lot behind the outfitter's beside Milly's car and got out. But the very sight of Milly smiling at him made whatever cautionary good sense he had vanish in a heartbeat.

And when she took his hand and said, "Come with me," he thought it was just as well it didn't matter that he didn't have much.

He was a goner.

Cash was here.

In her arms. In her life.

In her bed!

Not, for once, just in her dreams, which was where he'd been for months. Months, ha. Years is what it felt like.

"See?" she'd said when she brought him up. She'd opened the door and gestured at the small living room with its tall narrow windows.

"Uh-huh," Cash said.

Somewhere between appreciating the view of the drug store across the street and the book store down the block, he'd slid his hands under her shirt. Sometime after he'd admired the kitchen cupboards and the tiny apartment-sized stove that had been there at least sixty years, he undid her buttons and slipped the shirt off her shoulders. Somehow, when she was pointing out the brand-new carpeting, his mouth had found its way from her jaw to her shoulder to her nipple.

Milly had sucked in a sharp breath. "Cash!"

"Hmm?" He didn't lift his head. He didn't stop.

Milly wobbled. She clutched at his short dark hair and settled for grabbing his shoulders. "Cash! Stop!"

He raised his head, then, and looked at her, his blue eyes dark. "Stop?" He didn't sound as if he believed her.

She shook her head. She didn't believe her herself. "Don't stop," she whispered.

He hadn't.

He said, "How 'bout showin' me the bedroom, sweetheart?"

And Milly nodded her head toward the door on the far side of the kitchen. "Right through there."

She didn't think he paid much attention to the bedroom, even though he left the light on. His attention, as far as she could tell, was focused entirely on her. She'd almost shivered under the intensity of his gaze.

If his gaze didn't send her over the edge, the feel of his fingers on her heated skin certainly did. She was trembling by the time he'd rid her of her bra and then skimmed her jeans over her hips. Her fingers fumbled while she tried to undo his shirt and unfasten his Wranglers.

"I'll do it," he said, yanking his shirt off without regard to the buttons. When his hand covered hers at the fastening of his jeans, she felt a fine tremor running through him, too. He wasn't much better with the snap and the zipper than she was. But finally he got them shoved down to his knees and then realized he still had on his boots. Cursing, he struggled to get his boots off and fell onto the bed as he tried.

Milly laughed. "Let me." And she knelt at his feet and took hold of the heel, then gave a gentle pull. "Don't want to hurt your leg."

"M'leg's fine," Cash said. "Hurry up."

Milly tugged off one, then the other, and all the while Cash's fingers tangled in her hair. The minute his boots were off, he hauled her up, pulling her on top of him, rolling her beneath him on the bed, then raising himself up on his hands to look down at her. His eyes were dark as they looked her over, his pupils wide so that only a tiny rim of blue was visible around them.

"You are so beautiful," he breathed. His whole body seemed to be trembling now. He shoved himself back so that he rested on his knees between hers. His hands traced her shoulders, her breasts, her ribs. She sucked in a sharp breath. Then his fingers curled inside the elastic waistband of her panties and drew them down.

For an instant Milly seemed to freeze.

"What's wrong?" Cash asked softly.

She shook her head. "I don't...I'm not..." But she didn't finish.

"You are," he assured her. "You are everything."

"Dori says—"

"Don't want Dori." He'd never felt a moment's attraction to her sister. He didn't want anyone but her.

He didn't let her protest anymore. Knowing Milly, if he ever let her get started talking, they'd discuss it forever. Cash wasn't interested in discussing what he wanted right now. He slid the panties down her legs and tossed them aside. Then his hands came back at once to stroke her.

Milly shivered and squirmed under his touch. He smiled.

"Cash," she admonished.

"Mmm?" He bent and gave her a quick kiss on the lips, then pulled back to strip off his shorts.

Milly sucked in her breath. Her eyes got big as she looked at him.

"What?" Cash demanded, because he wasn't sure she didn't look horrified.

She smiled impishly. "Refrigerator magnets and art history classes don't do you justice," she said.

"*What?*"

She blushed. "I've never seen an...adult...um, male... er, on the hoof before."

Cripes. Now she had *him* blushing. "Don't look," he said gruffly.

"Oh, I want to look." She was looking actually quite

fascinated. With one of her fingers she reached out to touch him.

Cash shuddered.

She looked at him wide-eyed. "I didn't hurt you?"

He let out a shaky breath. "Babe, you are killin' me."

Milly jerked her hand away. "I'm sorry. I won't—I didn't—!" Her face burned.

"'S all right. 'S fine. More than fine. It's—hell, Milly, it's the best thing that ever was." He bit his lower lip. "It's just…been so damn long."

"Has it?" She smiled. "I'm glad."

That was women for you. They didn't want you to hurt. But they didn't want you feeling too good, either. They were downright perverse at times. Cash shook his head.

Milly reached to touch him again. He shook his head. "Not yet, darlin'. Let me…let me make it good for you."

"It's already good for me," Milly said softly, lowering her gaze.

"Yeah?" He smiled. "Well, let me make it better."

And then he touched her. His fingers found her, caressed her, stroked her. And she moaned. She twisted. Her fingers tightened on the comforter beneath her. "Cash!"

He grinned and settled alongside her. "Yes, darlin'? You like that?"

"Cash! What are you doing!" she demanded as he bent his head and kissed her stomach, nibbling on her exquisitely smooth skin. A trembling hand touched his ear, then dug into his hair. "Cash? I need you, Cash."

"And I need you," he whispered back raggedly, urgently.

"Then come to me," she urged.

"I will, babe," he said. But instead of doing so, he pulled away.

"Cash?"

He snagged his jeans off the floor and fished in the

pocket, taking out a tiny foil packet. "Did you know I was a Boy Scout, darlin'?" he asked her. His voice sounded strained even to his own ears, but he knew he needed to do this.

"Prepared?" Milly laughed a little when she saw the packet in his hand. "You're a wonder, Cash."

"The wonder is that I've lasted this long," he muttered. He was fumbling with the packet even as he spoke.

"Can I help?"

"I'll manage," he said through his teeth. But it took him longer than seemed possible because out of the corner of his eye he could see her there, waiting, eager for him, too.

He told himself to go slow, to be gentle. He tried. Dear God, he tried!

He told himself not to be disappointed if she felt more hurt than ecstasy. He knew it might not be the best sex in the world. He told himself he was going to go over the edge in scant seconds, no matter how hard he tried, because it had been so damn long his body wouldn't cooperate.

He never told himself that it would be wonderful.

But it was.

It was hot and urgent and wonderful beyond words. He took it as slow as he could. He touched her and kissed her and made her writhe with wanting him—though no more than he wanted her! And when he could hold out no longer, he let her take him in.

The feel of her body clenching around him drove him right over the edge, just as he'd known it would. But Milly seemed to be riding right along with him. And when her eyes opened wide and she gasped, "Oh my God!" he would have laughed if he'd been physically able.

He wasn't. He was shattered. He was spent. He collapsed against her and felt her arms go around him, holding him tight.

"Mil?" he whispered.

"I love you," she said.

Milly had dreamed of sharing like this with Cash, had imagined the intimate connection of their bodies, hearts and souls. But the reality of making love transcended even her dreams. What happened between them was the most intimate expression of feelings she could imagine.

If it wasn't perfect, she didn't know it. It shattered her and made her whole at the same time. After loving Cash, Milly knew that she would never be the same again.

She turned her head and kissed him. "I didn't think you were going to come back," she told him.

"Of course I was comin' back," he mumbled.

"You were mad."

"Yeah. For a little while. Then I broke my leg."

"And you couldn't come! Oh Cash!" She hugged him. "I didn't know! Why didn't you call?"

"You couldn't have done anything."

"I'd have tried. I'd do anything for you."

She felt his lips curve against her ear. "Anything?" he said, his voice low and roughly sexy.

"Anything," she agreed daringly.

He slid between her legs. "Then let's do this again."

The smell of bacon cooking woke him.

The smell of coffee closer at hand made his stomach growl. He twisted in the bed, knowing he was dreaming— he couldn't afford room service no matter how cheap it was—and opened his eyes.

"Good morning." Milly stood at the foot of the bed, smiling at him, holding a cup of coffee in her hand. "Here."

Cash shoved himself back against the headboard and took the coffee mug from her hand, amazed that he wasn't dreaming. But the cup was hot. He could hear the bacon sizzling. And Milly smelled like lilacs and something even more wonderful. And she was very definitely real.

He snagged her fingers with his other hand and drew her down beside him. "First you, then the coffee," he said, and then he kissed her. It began as a warm lazy kiss and ended, as he should have known it would, just short of a full-fledged forest fire.

He'd had her how many times last night—three? four?—and he still couldn't get enough of her. He set the coffee on the bedside table and pulled her into his arms.

Milly came to him as eagerly as she had every other time, kissing him back with a fervor that made his mind spin and his loins ache. He bore her down onto the bed and tugged at the tie of her robe.

"Cash," she whispered. "We can't."

"Of course we can."

"The bacon's burning."

"What?"

"The bacon! I'm cooking breakfast. I've got pancake batter made. The bacon's cooking. I need to turn it. I—"

He silenced her with his mouth. "Let it burn," he muttered.

And she might have, if the smoke alarm hadn't gone off.

At its insistent scream, Milly scrambled up and flew out of the room. Ruefully, Cash watched her go. He glanced at his watch. It was only seven-thirty. If they ate quick, they still might be able to manage a little more loving before he had to leave. Heartened, he hauled himself out of bed and padded toward the bathroom to shave.

Milly made more bacon. The first batch, she said, was burned beyond hope. And she had a stack of fluffy pancakes on a plate for him when he came out of the bathroom ten minutes later. "Orange juice or grapefruit?" she asked.

"Orange." He came up behind her and wrapped his arms around her as she poured it. The juice slopped on her hand.

"Cash," she protested. But she backed up against him at the same time. It wasn't the move of a woman who wanted him to leave her alone.

"Hmm?" He kissed her hair, her ear, the line of her jaw. "You're insatiable."

"Seems like," he agreed, still kissing.

Milly turned in his arms. "Your pancakes are going to get cold."

"I'll live," Cash murmured against her lips. "I don't want to live without this." And he led her back to the bedroom.

When he laid her on the bed, he did feel a momentary qualm however. Milly was a virgin. Or she had been, until she'd loved him all night.

Maybe he was asking too much of her to do it again this morning.

"Are you...okay?" he asked, feeling awkward and a little hesitant.

She blushed, then nodded her head and held out her arms to him.

Still feeling a little guilty for what seemed almost like taking advantage yet again, Cash went to her. "I want it to be good for you."

"It is good for me," she replied.

"The best," he insisted. "I want it to be the best."

And this time he concentrated even more on her. With the edge off his own rampant desire, he was able to be tender, to go slow, to take delight in her growing response, instead of just plunging on toward the main event. And when, at last, they joined, he was sure she was really with him this time, sharing, loving.

"Ah, yes!" The words were choked out of him as he fell into her embrace, and he was gratified when her body convulsed, her arms tightened around him, and she whispered, "Yessssss!" too.

Then the breath seemed to go right out of her, and she lay beneath him, totally spent.

Cash rolled off, but stayed next to her, still stroking her, letting his fingers trace the long line of her leg while his lips caressed her shoulder, her jaw. "Perfect," he murmured.

Milly's eyes opened. She turned her head. "Does this mean you don't want to do it anymore?"

Cash laughed. "Not for another ten or fifteen minutes, anyway."

"So we can eat?" Milly asked.

"So we can eat," Cash agreed. But even so he levered himself off the bed reluctantly. Then he glanced at his watch and winced. He should have been on the road by now. He had a lot of miles to cover to get to Oregon, where he was riding tomorrow afternoon.

"Like to take you with me," he grumbled, stuffing his shirt into his jeans and zipping them.

"I'd like to come." Milly wrapped her robe around her. "And I will when I can. But I can't leave yet. We should probably wait until Dad's a little better before we get married."

Get married?

Cash stopped dead, almost swallowing his tongue. He hadn't heard her right. He was *sure* he hadn't heard her right. She hadn't said, *married,* had she?

He looked at Milly as if she were some alien dropped into the middle of the bedroom. She was standing at the mirror running a brush through her long, tangled hair. She thought they were *getting married?*

The words sounded almost foreign. They sure as hell felt foreign. Hell, he couldn't remember ever having spoken them out loud in his life!

"Maybe it's better that you didn't come back earlier—as long as I wasn't going to Denver," she said, looking in the mirror and meeting his gaze. Deliberately and carefully he closed his gaping mouth. "I couldn't have left Dad in the lurch, you know."

Cash blinked. He wasn't capable of words.

"Of course I suppose we could have got married and I could have stayed here..." Her voice drifted off, and this time she did look at him, as if expecting him to have an answer.

He opened his mouth again, but the words still wouldn't come.

Milly smiled a little ruefully. "But it probably isn't the best way to start a marriage."

"Um...no." At least he managed that.

"Well, I can't really leave him yet. He's only working a couple of hours a day. But in a few months...you don't mind waiting a few months, do you? I mean, we've waited *this* long! It'll be hard, but I guess I can wait." She gave him an impish, conspiratorial smile, one that said she was totally unaware that she had just rocked the foundations of his world.

And that was when Cash realized that if he told her he hadn't any intention of getting married anytime soon—hadn't so much as given it a thought—he'd positively shatter hers.

He wasn't sure he actually *wasn't* going to marry Milly—sometime. Someday.

Just not now.

The very thought damn near gave him hives. It made the skin prickle on the back of his neck. It made him break out in a cold sweat. *Get married?* No sir. No way!

He just knew he wasn't ready for it. Heck, he'd barely turned twenty-eight. Milly was just twenty-three. They had their whole lives ahead of them! If they started now they could be married sixty years, for heaven's sake!

They didn't need to think about anything so permanent, so solid, so unrelenting—so damn terrifying—as marriage.

But he couldn't say so.

Not the way Milly was looking at him, her heart in her eyes.

He cleared his throat. He raked his fingers through his hair. He shifted from one foot to the other. His leg throbbed and he rubbed it instinctively. "Cripes, Milly, we don't have time to talk about things like that now." He glanced at his watch in desperation. "I gotta go."

"You haven't even eaten," she protested.

"Well, I don't have time to eat." He got the one boot on and reached for the other.

"It's ready, Cash. You need to eat."

"I'll grab somethin' on the road."

"But—"

"Don't worry. I won't starve." He jammed his heel down hard, wincing as he did so. But he had to go. He felt like the trap was closing. Grabbing Milly, he hauled her close and kissed her hard one last time. "Bye."

She hung on, hugged him. "Bye," she said against his lips. Her tongue touched his.

God, she was so-o-o-o tempting!

But she expected him to marry her.

"Oregon's callin', sweetheart." He untangled himself and backed rapidly toward the door, snagging his hat off the chair as he went.

Milly followed him out onto the porch. "I love you, Cash," she said as he clattered down the steps.

At the bottom he turned back and looked up at her smiling down at him. His heart did a funny sort of somersault. He swallowed. "Love you, too, Mil."

It was, after all, probably the truth.

Just not the whole truth—which was that the very thought of marrying her scared him to death.

She was a woman in love.

A woman committed.

She had given herself without reservation to Cash Callahan—mind and body, heart and soul.

She loved him.

He loved her.

She knew it. Not just because of his words. Not because of the need in him that night—or the desire or the passion. Most important, there had been reverence, too.

Cash Callahan loved her. Milly knew it.

It was just a matter of her father getting better and taking his place back at work. Then they could get married. She knew that, too.

She didn't see Cash again for a month. She knew he needed to go hard if he was going to make enough money to live on this year, now that there was no hope for him making the finals. She didn't mind. She'd waited without knowing he loved her, hadn't she?

This wait was easier by far.

And she didn't mind being the one to call him now. She didn't feel awkward using his pager number. They were in love, after all.

Besides, whenever she paged him, he called her right back. He told her about the horses he'd drawn, the rides he'd made. He talked fast and furious, hardly let her get a word in edgewise. When she did, she told him she loved him, and was pleased when he said he loved her, too. And then, of course, he always asked about her dad.

She guessed he was as eager as she was for them to tie the knot.

Her father's progress wasn't as fast as she'd hoped. "He tires so easily. I don't know when he'll be ready to come back full-time."

And because he was the kind, infinitely patient man he was, "Don't hurry him," Cash always said.

Milly loved him.

She said so often enough. But more than the words, there was the way she smiled at him, the way she touched him, the way she showed him her love whenever her body welcomed his.

He was the only man she'd ever made love with. He knew that, too. It made him feel warm and content and strong and kind of deep-down happy. It also scared him to death.

This love she was showing him and talking about was capital letter LOVE. No-holds-barred LOVE. The kind that had *marriage* written all over it. It fairly shouted the word—just as she did.

He knew she wanted it, expected it, had a right to it.

And still he couldn't bring himself to say it out loud.

He thought he would get better at it if he practiced. He and his new traveling partners, Denny and Walt, drove thousands of miles over hundreds of hours. And a lot of the time that they were driving, Cash said the word *marriage* over and over in his head.

It didn't help.

In fact, the more often he thought about it, the worse he felt.

He had nothing to offer a woman in marriage. He had no home, no steady income, no prospects beyond the next eight-second ride. He hadn't won the world. He wasn't even going to make it to the finals this year. He'd be lucky if he didn't have to take a construction job to get through the winter.

"Reckon you're washed up?" his old man asked when Cash called home to wish them a merry Christmas. Len Callahan felt about the word *tact* what Cash did about *marriage*.

"No," Cash said through his teeth.

Len grunted. "Better be checkin' out a real job."

Not on your life, Cash thought. That was one more step down the road to being exactly what his old man was. "Merry Christmas to you, too," he said, and hung up.

He went back to bed with Milly.

"It'll be better next year," she told him.

"Gotta be," he said, wrapping her in his arms.

"You'll make it. It will be your lucky year."

"Mmm." Kissing her made it feel better already.

"Dad's so much stronger. I think by summer I can leave him. Just think," she snuggled closer. "By this time next year we'll be married!"

Cash swallowed and covered her mouth with his. He didn't want to talk about that.

Milly did.

As time went by, Cash thought she had weddings on the brain.

All her friends were making plans. Why weren't they?

"We could get married in the summer," she told him when he came through in March. They were lying in bed, wrapped in each other's arms.

Cash shook his head. "Summer's my busiest time."

"It doesn't take long. One afternoon."

"Plannin' takes long." He'd heard nothing but wedding plans every time he'd seen her in the past two months.

"I'll do it. You don't have to do anything but show up."

He sat up and reached for his shorts. "We aren't in any hurry, you know." He glanced back over his shoulder at her.

Milly blinked. "We aren't?"

"Well, I'm not," he admitted finally, standing up and pulling on his jeans.

Milly sat up. Her eyes widened. "You're not?"

He shrugged awkwardly and slipped into his shirt. "Well, it's not a real big deal, is it? I mean, what's marriage really? What would we have that we don't have now?'' He gave her his best cowboy grin.

Milly didn't grin back. "We'd have commitment," she told him. "Vows."

Exactly what he was afraid of. Cash buttoned his shirt, then scratched the back of his head. "Commitment," he said. Another one of those foreign terms. "Um, well—" he glanced at his watch "—oops. Gotta go."

He kissed her quickly and left while she was still getting dressed.

He stayed away a month this time. He had a slew of rodeos to go to down south. They paid better than the ones up north, he told her on the phone. He needed time—and space—and so did she—enough to get the whole marriage bug out of her system.

He didn't get back until a Friday afternoon in May. He went to the store, hoping he would find Dori there with her so Dori could be backup while he spirited Milly away for a little quick loving.

Instead he found John there by himself. "She's at home," Milly's father said.

Cash's eyes widened. "You're back full-time?"

John lifted his shoulders a fraction of an inch. "Gettin' there."

"Great." Which it was—unless it gave Milly ideas.

And he could see it had when he used the key she'd given him to let himself into her apartment ten minutes later. She was pirouetting around the room in a wedding dress!

He almost dropped dead.

Milly did, too, but from astonishment, not sheer terror. "Isn't it gorgeous?" she said when she recovered. "It's Lizzie Thomas's. I told her I'd hem it for her."

Cash felt as if his tongue was welded to the roof of his

mouth. The vision of Milly in yards and yards of white satin did nothing to loosen it.

"I'm hemming my dress, too," Milly said. "See?" She held up the deep blue bridesmaid's dress lying on the table.

Cash nodded mutely.

"I think I'd like blue at our wedding, too. What do you think?" Milly asked.

"I haven't thought about it." Didn't *want* to think about it.

Cash had other, far more pleasurable things to think about—Milly naked beneath him, Milly eager to love him, Milly asleep in his arms.

He reached for her.

She slipped out of his grasp. "Careful of the dress. Maybe not such a vivid blue, though."

"Whatever. Turn around." He meant to dispose of the dress as quickly as he could. "I've missed you."

"I missed you, too," Milly said. She turned and bent her head and he set to work on the top button. His fingers fumbled. He cursed.

Milly giggled. "I'll have to remember not to have buttons on mine."

Cash didn't answer. He unzipped her and eased the dress off her shoulders. Carefully Milly stepped out of it, then hung it up and stood for just a moment, looking at it wistfully.

"Come here," Cash said, catching her hand and drawing her toward him and away from the wedding dress.

Milly came willingly then. She wrapped her arms around him and kissed him, then took him into the bedroom and loved him—and the subject of marriage didn't come up again.

Until the next morning.

"Dad's doing much better," she said from the bedroom, while Cash stood in the bathroom shaving. "He's working full days three times a week. Between him and Dori they can pretty much cover things now.''

"Good for him.'' Cash kept his eyes strictly on his own face in the mirror. He didn't glance to see if she was peering at him from the doorway.

"So we can set a date.'' Her voice drifted in to him.

Cash turned the water on, splashing it loudly, drowning her out. He hummed.

"Did you hear me, Cash?'' Her voice came more loudly. "We can set a date.''

"Date?'' he mumbled into a mouthful of shaving soap.

Milly poked her head around the door and looked at him in the mirror. Their eyes met. His shifted quickly away.

For a moment Milly didn't speak. Then, "We can talk about it when you finish,'' she said quietly and left.

"You don't want to talk about the wedding at all, do you?''

He'd considered a dozen ways to avoid this conversation. He knew none of them would work. They stared at each other over the pancakes, and Cash knew they'd reached the moment of truth.

Cash shrugged. "Not 'specially.'' He tried to sound casually indifferent, not negative. He bent his head and concentrated on his breakfast. He wouldn't have to talk if his mouth was full.

Unfortunately Milly's mouth was not. And it was a subject she was determined to pursue. "Why not?''

Deliberately he finished chewing, then swallowed, hoping all the while she'd go on to say something else. She didn't. She waited. Finally he was forced to answer. "'Cause we got plenty of time to get married,'' he said irritably. "I told you that.''

"Don't you *want* to get married?''

He stabbed a pancake. "Sure. Someday." He took another mouthful.

"Someday?"

He nodded. "Someday." He couldn't be any more definite than that.

"We're not getting any younger," Milly said finally.

"We're not that old! I'm twenty-eight! You're only twenty-three!"

That didn't seem to matter to Milly. "Someday we'll be glad we got married as young as we did. At least we'll be spry enough to run after our kids."

Kids?

She thought he was old enough to be a *father?* Cash almost choked.

Milly didn't notice. "In fact, we're not all that young anymore, really," she went on reflectively. She wrapped her hands around her coffee mug and looked at him over the top.

"Lots of folks don't get married till they're past thirty," he told her stubbornly.

"Thirty?" Milly yelped. The coffee sloshed out of her mug as she jumped to her feet and glared down at him. "You think I want to watch you come and go like I've got a swinging door on my place until you're *thirty?*"

"I wasn't thinking of me," Cash protested. "I was thinking of you."

He thought later it might have been a mistake to be so honest.

She practically threw him out the door!

Nine

"Women," Cash told Dennis and Walt that night as they rolled down the highway toward Tucson, "are a pain in the neck."

Denny grinned and flexed his shoulders and stretched. "I'd have said they hit a damn sight lower myself. But yeah, I know what you mean."

"They're never satisfied," Cash went on. "They always want somethin' else."

"A new dress. A box of chocolates. Pretty flowers," Walt said. "A gold buckle with your name on it."

"A wedding ring," Cash said grimly.

Both men's eyes jerked wide. "Oh, hell. Like that, is it?" Denny said.

Cash sighed. "Like that."

"You didn't do it?" Walt asked fervently.

Cash shook his head. "'Course not. I'm not gettin' shackled. She's crazy if she thinks I'm ready to settle down and be some little lap dog."

"Damn right," Dennis agreed. They all stared at the white line stretching before them, in silent contemplation of matrimony. Cash thought Walt actually shuddered. He'd done some trembling himself, ever since his argument with Milly that morning.

It had been a stupid argument. They never should have had it. She should have known better than to push him. It wasn't like he'd ever asked her to marry him, was it?

No.

She was being presumptuous. Assuming things that he'd never said. Making plans based on fantasies, not reality. So she was wrong, right?

Right.

And Milly was reasonable. She would see that she was wrong. If he just waited a little while, gave her a chance to cool off, permitted her an opportunity to reflect on things, she'd come to see things his way. It wasn't as if he had said he was *never* going to marry her.

Of course he'd probably marry her—when he got ready to get married.

Someday.

"She'll get over it," he said to himself as much as to his buddies. "She'll be fine next time I stop."

"Give her some time," Denny counseled. "Don't go runnin' right back to make up with her."

"Hell, no."

He called her on the phone once. She didn't think they had anything to talk about.

Fine, he thought. They'd sort it out in person. He gave her two months. He stopped by one night on his way from Nebraska to Alberta. It was out of his way. Denny and Walt had flown with some buddies, and Cash probably should have, too, but he'd been thinking about Milly a lot.

Missing her, if the truth were known, and he thought by now maybe she'd cooled off.

At least he hoped so. He climbed the steps to her apartment and stuck his key in the lock.

It didn't turn.

"What the—?" He tried it again. He pulled it out and looked at it, certain that he had the right key, but thinking maybe he'd just poked in the wrong one in his hurry.

He jiggled it again, twisted the knob. Nothing happened.

He frowned and banged on the door. Her car was in the lot, so she had to be home. "Milly!" He banged again. "Hey, Milly! It's me. Open up."

When she finally opened the door, he was amazed. She had her hair pulled up in a red ribbon and tied in some fancy ridiculous knot! Cash reckoned he could make quick work of that ribbon!

"What the heck's goin' on?" he asked. "Things gettin' so urban you had to change the lock?"

"No. I didn't want you barging in."

He stared at her, shocked.

"And I don't have time to talk to you now, either," she said. She picked up her purse and hugged it against her breasts. "I have a date."

"A *date?*" His brows drew down. "What do you mean, you have a date?" *How the hell could she have a date? She was his girl!*

"I have a date," Milly repeated firmly. "I just got home from work about half an hour ago. I'm in a hurry. So, please excuse me."

"The hell I'll *excuse* you! What do you mean, you're goin' out on a date? You can't go out on a date. You're marryin' me!"

"No," Milly said. "I'm not. You never asked me to marry you."

"Never stopped you assumin' before," Cash snapped.

"My mistake. Obviously," Milly said, green eyes flashing. "And now I realize it. I'm sure you're happy to know that."

"Well, of course I'm happy, but—" Cash began, relieved and annoyed as hell at the same time. Yeah, she was supposed to realize it, but she wasn't supposed to use it as an excuse to date some other guy, for heaven's sake!

"So, you are free, too. Now let me past. Goodbye."

"But—"

"Go."

"No."

They glared at each other. Cash's jaw clenched. Milly's lips pressed into a hard, tight line.

"What guy?" he asked after a moment. He needed to know whose block to knock off.

"You don't know him."

"What's his name?"

Milly tipped her chin. "His name is Mike Dutton."

"Where'd you meet him? How do you know he's somebody you should be spending any time with?"

"There's a laugh," Milly said scornfully. "After all the time I spent on you. I should get a medal for smartening up. Mike is a solid, dependable, responsible man with a steady full-time job, who is looking to settle down. He's a CPA."

Cash's teeth came together with a snap. A *CPA?* She was dumping him for a *number cruncher?*

"Sounds boring as hell to me."

"He would to you. To me he's a breath of fresh air. And I'm intending to enjoy it. Now, I really must be going." She stepped out and shut the door firmly behind her. "Goodbye, Cash."

And damned if she didn't brush right past him down the stairs!

Milly didn't realize how badly she was shaking until she got into her car. She actually needed the anchor of the steering wheel to stop trembling. Her stomach was doing somersaults even then, but there was no help for that.

There was no help at all except turning on the engine and getting away from Cash as quickly as she could.

She'd told herself she could handle seeing him. She knew she *would* see him—"someday," as he so blithely intended everything to happen in their relationship—and she'd promised herself she'd be prepared.

Prepared had meant talking hours on end to Dori and her friend Poppy about the mistakes she'd made. It had meant talking herself out of making any more mistakes where Cash was concerned.

She knew she'd been a fool. She had, as she'd just told him, assumed too much. *Way* too much. He'd wanted the long-term equivalent of a roll in the hay—and nothing more.

She didn't know whether she was more angry or hurt or embarrassed at her own naïveté. But she was done being a fool in any case.

She wasn't letting it happen again. She'd changed the locks. She'd steeled herself for the inevitable confrontation. She *hadn't* cried.

She'd been prepared.

Sort of.

Basically she knew she would never be prepared to deal with Cash—not like this. She either needed to be married to him—or she needed him out of her life.

"Those cowboys," her mother had said grimly. "I'd reckoned he was different. There aren't *any* of 'em any good."

"Oh, Mom, there must be one," Dori had said, though heaven knew her own experience had certainly given them no cause to believe it.

"One," Milly had echoed miserably.

Just not the one she loved.

"The best thing," Dori had advised, "is not to sit home. You need to get out, meet people. Meet *men*," she said more firmly, before Milly could tell her she was going to the garden club meeting with Poppy the Wednesday after next.

"Men?"

"I'll introduce you," Dori said firmly. Even though she wasn't dating anyone, she seemed to know every man who passed through Livingston in particular and southern Montana in general.

Milly hadn't been enthusiastic. But Dori had been firm. She'd pushed Milly into going to local baseball games and to picnics sponsored by the outfitter downstairs, to church socials and to fly fishing tournaments.

"You canoe. We'll find you a canoer."

"Canoeist," Milly corrected.

"Whichever. A man," Dori said.

"I don't want another man," Milly protested.

"You don't have to marry him. You just need to get your mind off Cash."

To Milly's surprise, Dori's prescription worked. It was hard to spend her every waking moment thinking about him when she was in the company of other men.

They were nice men, too—most of them. Especially measured against a certain rodeo cowboy.

And one of the nicest things about them all was that they weren't Cash.

Milly didn't need any more feckless roaming cowpokes. She didn't need any more men who would ride off into the sunset at the drop of a hat. She didn't need any more males whose staying power was something short of the ten-second mark.

"Eight, to be exact," Dori said.

Well, in a word, yes.

At first Milly told herself that she was just using these men to keep thoughts of Cash at bay. But eventually she realized that one, at least, was worth another look for himself, and not just because he wasn't Cash.

Mike Dutton was lean and blond and handsome in his own less lethal way. That was appealing for starters. He didn't physically bear any resemblance to Cash. But he was also quietly determined.

He called her when he said he would. He came in the store and talked to her. He asked her to go to the movies and to concerts in Billings. He took her to an art exhibit in Bozeman, and to a coffee house to hear a reggae group.

He didn't seem to mind when she stopped in the middle of sentences or stared off into space sometimes, caught in a time warp of remembering Cash.

He was patient. He had staying power.

Milly liked staying power. She liked Mike.

A good thing, too, because seeing Cash again so unexpectedly today had rattled her down to her toes.

She had told Mike she would meet him at his office because it was on the way to Bozeman where they were going to a movie. She practically flew at him when she got out of the car.

"Hey!" He grabbed her and hugged her close. "What's up?"

"N-nothing. J-just glad to see you." Her teeth were chattering, and it was summer, for heaven's sake!

Still holding her, he nodded. "Cash in town?"

Her head jerked up. "What?" She felt her face burn and wondered if Mike could see that, too. From the look on his face, she knew that he could. "I'm sorry," she said miserably.

"Me, too," he said, his tone a little grim.

"I told him to leave," she said. "I practically knocked him over on my way down the stairs."

Mike's brows lifted. A ghost of a grin flickered across his face. "Did you? I'd liked to have seen that."

"He's a jerk," Milly said.

Mike grunted and led her to his car, tucking her into it, then he went around and got in beside her. He took her hand and looked into her eyes. "He's a fool. I'll say that."

Obviously she needed more time.

Women were like that. They didn't realize right off that love wasn't just promises and wedding dresses. But Milly was sharp. She'd figure it out eventually.

She probably just had a bee in her bonnet since he didn't knuckle under and go down on one knee and propose just because she thought he ought to. Well, okay, he could be tolerant—to a point—as long as it didn't take her too long to wake up and remember who really loved her.

Next time he came through, Cash assured himself, things would be fine.

He made it a point to come back to Livingston sooner than he might have otherwise. He didn't want to make her wait too long. He thought she ought to have a chance to apologize pretty quick. It would eat at her otherwise.

This time he didn't try his key. He even knocked politely and waited. Her car was there, so she had to be home.

Probably she was washing her hair or maybe she was in the shower, he thought, when his first knock wasn't answered within a decent amount of time. He knocked again. Maybe she had the stereo turned up so she couldn't hear him. But he couldn't hear any music. He just heard himself banging.

"Milly!"

Where the hell was she? It was seven o'clock on a Saturday night. She wouldn't be at the store now. He banged again. Louder.

There was a sound on the steps behind him. He turned

to see a middle-aged man in yuppie camper gear. "You know where Milly is?" Cash asked.

"She went to Seattle."

"Seattle?" Cash frowned. "Why?"

The man shrugged. "Dunno. She just asked me to take in her mail. She'll be gone over the weekend. Went with her boyfriend."

Boyfriend?

"What boyfriend?" Cash demanded.

The yuppie backed down a step. "Er, blond guy. Name's Mike, I think."

"Mike." Cash fairly spat the name. "She went *for the weekend?*"

"That's what she said. Want me to tell her you came by?"

"No." Cash barked the word. He clattered down the steps and brushed past the man, jumped into his truck and burned rubber on his way down the street.

Seattle? Boyfriend? Weekend?

What the hell did Milly think she was doing?

He'd cleared his whole evening to be with her. He figured her apology would take maybe five minutes and they could put the rest of the time to good use getting "reacquainted." He wasn't planning to leave until tomorrow at ten. And now not only wasn't he going to get an apology—she wasn't even home!

He practically sideswiped a Suburban wheeling into the parking lot outside a local watering hole. The man in the Suburban yelled at him. Cash yelled back and made a rude gesture besides. He banged the door to his truck, headed straight into the bar and finished the night right there.

The bartender peeled him off his stool at closing time. "Let me find you a ride."

"Got m'truck."

"You're in no shape to drive."

"I ain't goin' nowhere," Cash gave a vague wave of his hand and wobbled carefully out the door to make his way to his truck.

He slept in the truck. It wasn't the first time. It probably wouldn't be the last.

But the combination of alcohol and cramped sleeping quarters and faithless women didn't do a lot for his frame of mind or body.

When the sun blinded him awake the next morning, he felt like a herd of elk wearing horseshoes and brandishing whiskey bottles had done disgusting things to his body and to his head.

He found a café and used the bathroom, sticking his head under the faucet and keeping it there until the drum roll in his brain got so intense he felt like throwing up. Then he jerked his head up and took great lungfuls of air, shuddering and gasping and trying for sanity and sobriety and a whole lot of things that had been eluding him lately.

He stared at his bleary reflection in the cracked mirror over the sink. He was sallow-cheeked and sunken-eyed, his whiskery features relentlessly grim. It was a face not even a mother could love—let alone Milly.

Didn't she love him anymore?

The thought he'd done his best to keep at bay wouldn't be denied any longer. *Didn't she love him?*

She had to. He couldn't imagine that she didn't. But then—why had she gone with Dutton?

He tried to think rationally. Not easy. Logic had never been Cash's strong suit. But maybe there was a logical reason for Milly going to Seattle with her reliable accountant. Maybe they were studying urban bookkeeping methods, or he was advising her on stocking a new product line.

That sounded reasonable. Yeah, it really did. Cash felt a glimmer of hope. He rubbed a hand over his whiskers. If he shaved them off he'd feel more like coping and less like lying down and dying right where he was.

He shaved them off. Then he combed his hair and set his hat back on his head. His clothes still looked slept in, but he had a clean shirt he'd been planning to wear for the rodeo tonight. He'd turn his horse out and put on his clean shirt and stick around. He'd go sit in the parking lot in his truck until she and her number-cruncher got back tonight.

After all, there was no sense in imagining the worst. And he really did want to hear Milly's rational, logical, reasonable explanation for having gone to Seattle for the weekend with another man. There had to be one.

There was, Milly assured him coolly when she and Dutton tooled into the lot at quarter past nine that evening.

Cash scowled at her. "I'd like to know what," he said sharply.

"We got engaged."

Engaged?

He couldn't believe it.

How the hell could she do something so damn dumb? She loved *him*, damn it, not some solid, dependable, accountant Dutton jerk!

Cash ranted. He raved. He banged and crashed. Dutton watched him with the fascination of someone witnessing a car wreck. Milly didn't react at all except to say quietly to her fiancé—*fiancé!*—that there was no use in his staying.

"Damn right there isn't!" Cash snarled at him.

Dutton didn't look convinced. "He looks—"

"He looks worse than he is," Milly said. "I'll handle it."

Cash stood there with his mouth opening and closing, like some beached fish. "Handle what? You'll handle what?" he demanded.

"You," Milly said. She put a hand on Dutton's arm. She

was wearing a damned ring! Cash could see it winking in the light from the street lamp. His fingers balled into a fist. "It's all right," she said to Dutton.

"The hell it is," Cash growled.

"I don't—" Dutton began.

But Milly looked at him imploringly. "Please. He'll only behave worse if you stay."

Like he was some obnoxious child. Cash wanted to smash something.

Dutton looked doubtful, then nodded reluctantly and got back into his car. "Call me later. Or I'll call you."

Milly nodded.

Neither of them would be talking to the other, if Cash had anything to say about it. He'd yank the damn phone cord first!

He didn't say so. He didn't say anything else until Dutton had driven away. Then he turned on Milly, "What the hell is going on?"

"Nothing that concerns you." She started up the steps.

Cash went after her. "How can you say that? You love me!"

"I thought I did. But then, I thought you loved me, too." She didn't stop, she didn't even turn around.

"I *do* love you, damn it, Milly!"

"But you don't want to get married."

"Is that what this is all about? Getting married? You want to get married so bad you'd marry just any guy on the street?"

She turned then, and looked as if he'd slapped her. "No, I would not, as you put it, 'marry just any guy on the street.' I'd only marry one man—a man I loved."

"You love me," Cash insisted.

"*Did* love you. And I'd have married you! Once." She opened the door to her apartment. He came after her.

"Don't," she said. "Go away. I'm tired. I want to go to bed."

He'd thought nothing she could say would make him angrier—until she said that. *I'm tired. I want to go to bed.*

"Why? Didn't you get enough sleep with Dutton?"

Milly's cheeks flamed, exactly as he'd known they would. But it wasn't near the satisfaction he'd hoped for. The very thought of her sleeping with another man infuriated him more than it embarrassed her.

"What would you do," he asked her, "if I just walked right past you and went into the bedroom and lay down on your bed and waited for you?"

"Call the police."

And the firm, unblinking expression in her eyes was so unlike the Milly he knew that he couldn't be sure she didn't mean it. He couldn't say that she damned well wouldn't.

"Would you?" he finally snarled. Then he turned on his boot heel and stalked out.

Milly didn't even realize she was holding her breath until the last sound of the truck's engine died away. Then she took a deep, shuddering gulp of air and let it out slowly.

It would be better now.

She had set her course, turned her back on the past, made her peace with the future.

It was true what Cash had said. She had loved him. But a girl only had one life—and Milly didn't intend to spend hers sacking groceries and doing ledgers and watching Cash blow in and out of her life while he came to his senses.

She didn't think Cash had any sense. If he had, they'd have been married long ago.

No, she was doing the right thing marrying Mike.

As the weeks went by she told herself that a dozen times

a day. More than a dozen. A hundred. Lots. Dori told her, too. So did her mother. And her dad.

"Mike's a great guy."

"Mike's dependable."

"Mike's everything a girl could want in a husband."

He was. Milly knew that. But he was also, a niggling little voice inside told her, everything that Cash had said he was, too.

Cash heard, through the grapevine, that the wedding was in January.

He didn't care. It didn't matter to him. He'd be down south in January where it was warm and wonderful. After the Denver Stock Show, he was going to see his parents. He'd mosey on down to Houston and be ready when the livestock show opened there the following week.

That was a long, long way from Livingston, Montana. It might as well be on the other side of the moon.

It was so far away that, the longer Cash thought about it, he figured he might not hear when she backed out. The news might not reach him, and he might not be there to comfort her—not just to say "I told you so," which he damned well intended to do, too—when she came to her senses and broke things off.

That would be too bad.

He still liked Milly. Still had kind feelings toward her. Still thought of her as a friend. And she would need him then.

She needed him now. She just didn't seem to know it.

Cash guessed he could swing by Livingston after Denver, hang around a few days, then make his way south.

"You're out of your mind," Dennis told him. "All that way?"

"Reckon I ought to stop and see Shane. He's probably pretty grim about now." Cash had heard about the freak accident that had torn off Shane Nichols's thumb. He'd had it sewn back on again, but he couldn't ride for a while. And Cash knew all about enforced immobility. It didn't do a guy's mind good. He could stop in, cheer Shane up. It would be the friendly thing to do.

Better than having Milly think he'd come all that way for her, too.

"I'll just stay up there a few days. Maybe get in some skiing."

"Skiing?" Walt's eyes lit up. "I ain't been skiin' all year. How 'bout we come, too?"

It wasn't that far from Bridger and Big Sky. Skiing and seeing Shane—yeah, those were reasonable excuses for being in the neighborhood—if she asked. He didn't think she would. She'd probably be too glad to cry on his shoulder to even think about things like that.

It was a hell of a shock to get there and discover she was still planning to go through with it!

He'd looked for her at the grocery first, and had been surprised to have her dad tell him she'd quit.

"*Quit?*"

"She's working for Poppy Hamilton now, over at the florist's shop. She and I lock horns too often. Milly is a force."

Milly? A force? She used to be sweet and kind and caring. A naive little innocent who did what she could to please. What happened to *that* Milly? How come she was "a force" all of a sudden?

John Malone's mouth tipped in his version of a smile. "Life has a way of doing that to a person. All I know is she's stubborn as a wrong-headed mule."

Cash thought so, too.

He went to the florist's shop. Milly was there, but she pretty much ignored him. If he didn't want to order flowers, she had nothing to say.

"Tell me why you're still marryin' him," Cash said. But she turned her back to chop the heads off some yellow flowers. Cash had similar designs on hers.

He prowled around the florist's until Milly got off work, then he followed her home through the snow.

"Go away, Cash," she said, when he dogged her steps to her apartment.

"You can't be serious."

"Serious? What would you know about serious?" She slapped her hands on her hips. "You've *played* your entire adult life—*if* you can even call it adult!"

"I risk my neck at least a couple of times a week!" Cash retorted, stung. "I'm ridin' Deliverance on Saturday. He's a ball breaker. Nastiest horse this side of Hades."

"Then you're well matched." She started up the steps.

Cash glared at her back. Damn but she was stiff-necked. He raked a hand through his hair. He rubbed the back of his neck. "I came back 'cause I cared, Milly," he said at last.

She didn't even turn around.

He took the steps two at a time after her. "Damn it, did you hear me? I said, I care!"

"Enough not to ride on Saturday?"

He stopped. He frowned. "What?"

"You heard me." She stood, back against her door, and faced him. "Would you not ride if I asked you?"

"What do you mean, not ride? Why shouldn't I ride? If I stick on Deliverance, I'll make a pile. I'll be way up in the standings right from the start. He's a great horse. The best."

"Right." Milly stuck her key in the door.

Cash caught her arm and turned her around. "Right? What the hell does that mean?"

"Exactly what I said. It means your priorities haven't changed a bit."

He gaped at her. "It's my life. It's what I do. It's a life-and-death split-second business I'm in. The way I stay alive."

Milly nodded. "I know."

"So, what are you saying? Give it up? Don't ride? Be a damn grocer?" He couldn't help it; he practically spat the word at her.

She didn't flinch. "Of course not. Be anything you please. I'm just saying that it's the only thing that matters to you."

"You matter, damn it!"

"No. Going down the road matters. Being 'free' matters."

"Freedom is good," Cash said stubbornly.

"Fine, enjoy it, then, damn it. You're free!"

"I don't want to be free of *you!*" he argued.

"You don't want to get married."

It always came back to that.

"Hell. I—well, I—cripes, it's only until Tuesday, Milly!" He snatched off his hat and raked his fingers through his hair. "I could be back by Tuesday. We can talk about marriage on Tuesday!"

"We've had years to talk about marriage, Cash. You don't *want* to talk about it."

No, he didn't. He wasn't ready. But for her, he would.

"Tuesday," he muttered again.

"Tuesday I'll be on my honeymoon." She turned the knob, shoved open the door and went into her apartment. Cash followed her.

"Damn it, Milly. It's only three days."

She stopped and looked at him. "This is not about days, Cash. It's about years. You think in terms of eight seconds when you think about sticking with something. That won't work here. I don't want seconds. I don't want days. I want years. I want commitment. I want the long haul, and I can't pretend I don't.'' She paused and met his gaze squarely. "So I don't want you. I want Mike. Now, goodbye.''

Then she took Cash by the shoulders, turned him around and shoved him out the door.

Ten

The "something old" was her grandmother's wedding veil. The "something new" was the tiny pearl necklace her parents had given her on her engagement. The "something borrowed" was Dori's pair of white satin pumps that were at this very moment squeezing Milly's toes.

The "something blue" would not be her mood. Milly was determined about that.

She was happy. She was getting married in less than an hour. She loved Mike. And Cash had finally left town.

She hadn't thought he was *ever* going to leave!

The first time he'd turned up and she'd changed the locks, she'd believed he would go away and never come back. When she'd come home from Seattle and found him parked by her apartment, she'd thought that the news of her engagement would get rid of him once and for all.

When he turned up at Poppy's shop earlier this week, she couldn't believe it. Didn't he know what *no* meant?

What was he trying to do to her?

It wasn't as if he'd changed. He just wanted her here when he wanted to drop by and play house. Marriage? He acted like it was a jail sentence or something.

He was only willing to "talk" about it. And even then only on Tuesday after he'd finished riding his damned horse!

"Tuesday." She almost spat the word.

No way. Milly knew Cash. On Tuesday he'd be just as footloose and noncommittal as he'd always been.

She was desperately glad she'd been able to steel herself against him, relieved that she'd fought back, convinced she was doing the right thing.

But even then he hadn't gone!

He'd actually had the gall to show up at The Barrel two nights ago and glare at her! As if she was making the mistake—as if she was the one doing something wrong!

Well, fine. Let him glare.

Let him come back Tuesday.

She would be long gone—off to Mexico with Mike for a warm, winter honeymoon.

In any case, she wasn't going to think anymore about Cash. He was the past. She had real problems in the present.

Poppy, ordinarily the most reliable of friends, hadn't shown up to do the flowers! They'd taken the dried flowers to the church last night, and Poppy had said she'd come back and do the fresh ones this morning.

But when Dori had gone to help her, Poppy wasn't there.

"What do you mean, not there?" Milly had demanded. "Poppy is as predictable as the tides."

"Well, the tide has gone out apparently," Dori replied.

And she was telling the truth. The flowers were still in the cooler at the shop where they had left them yesterday.

Poppy was nowhere to be found.

Milly transported and arranged them herself.

In retrospect she realized that she should have known then that things were falling apart.

If the florist slept in—or totally forgot—or boycotted the wedding, well, what chance did you have that anything would go right?

But Milly was just so glad to be rid of Cash she wasn't thinking sensibly. Determined to focus not on the past—or on the future—but just on the present, she did what had to be done.

After the flowers were set, she came home and fixed her own hair. She tied her father's black bow tie and straightened his cummerbund.

"You look very handsome," she told him.

He grumbled a little, muttered about the tie strangling him.

"You'll survive," Milly told him. "You've survived worse than this."

In fact she thought he looked wonderful. He'd come back well from his heart attack. He was working every day now, but Dori was working almost as much now that Jake, at seven, was in school full-time.

Milly was amazed at how well they worked together after all the arguing they'd done in the past.

"We just had to come to terms," Dori said.

Milly was glad they'd done that.

"We wouldn't have, if you hadn't been here to shoulder the burden when Dad first got sick," Dori told her. "You gave up a lot."

Sometimes Milly thought Dori worried about her—about her not having gone to Denver, about what had happened with Cash.

But Cash wouldn't have married her, even if she'd gone to Denver. She knew that now. She'd just been too young and dumb to realize it earlier.

"I'm not sorry," Milly had told Dori more than once. It was little enough compared to the lifetime of love her father had given her. She was just glad she'd been able to return a small share.

She knew he appreciated it even if he never said much. Her mother did, too.

Her mother was worrying about her, too, wondering even as late as last week if Milly might be making a mistake. Her mother liked Mike. In the beginning she'd even lobbied for Mike. But she knew how much Milly had loved Cash.

"Are you sure you shouldn't wait for him?" she'd asked just last week.

"I can't wait for Cash. I might wait forever. I don't have forever, Mom. You only get one go-round in life."

And her mother had had to agree with that. She'd smiled gently, a little sadly, and kissed her daughter. "Good luck," she'd whispered.

"Good luck," Dori said as the music started.

Her father patted her hand. "Good luck," he whispered.

Even Jake, the reluctant ring bearer, said, "Good luck," right before Milly walked down the aisle.

That she didn't get it should have come as no big surprise.

He wasn't going to make it.

He *had* to make it.

He could barely see the taillights ahead of him. The world had dissolved into a huge white globe. Mark's "winter storm" had arrived with a vengeance. Cash had been battling it since just north of Cheyenne. They'd closed the highway north of Casper. He couldn't believe it.

"I can't stop!" he'd told the Highway Patrol, for all the good it did. "I'll take full responsibility," he assured them. "Let me go on!"

They just looked at him.

He cooled his heels, literally and figuratively, for six hours in Casper. Finally when the winds let up and the plows could make a difference, they opened the road. It was slow going. Time was getting short.

Damn it! What if he wasn't in time to stop her?

He had rented a car when Denny dropped him off. It was a Texas car, not equipped for the rigors of a Montana winter storm. Cash himself wasn't equipped for the rigors of a Montana winter storm. It didn't matter. He didn't stop.

West of Billings things got nasty again. He could barely see. He should have had chains. He had prayer and determination—and not much else.

The wedding was scheduled for eleven. He got there at quarter after. He parked his truck in front—pulled right up behind the car that had been decorated with "JUST MARRIED" on the back window and festooned with bright blue crepe paper streamers—and jumped out.

He took the steps to the church two at a time, yanked open the door and burst in.

The usher standing in the doorway between the vestibule and the sanctuary turned around and put his finger to his lips. "They've already begun," he said in a whisper. "I'll seat you in the back. Bride or groom?"

"Bride," Cash said. "But not his! Mine." He pushed past the usher, determined to get to Milly. He could see her. She stood with her back to him as she held hands with Mike and looked up at the minister.

"Stop!" The usher wasn't whispering now.

Half the congregation turned around. Cash heard mutters and titters. He didn't give a damn. He didn't stop, either.

Not until the usher grabbed his arm when he was halfway down the aisle. "Come back here! You can't do that!"

Everyone turned then. Even Milly. And the sight of her in a bridal gown that was her own this time was the final straw.

"I'd like to see you try and stop me," he said to the usher who foolishly tried to do just that.

Cash's fist shot out. A lady shrieked. The congregation gasped. The usher crumpled. And Cash stepped over him, determined to get to Milly.

She was staring straight at him, a horrified look on her face.

"You wouldn't wait till Tuesday," he said.

Her eyes grew as big as dinner plates. Her mouth opened and shut, but no words came out.

Mike said something harsh under his breath. Cash didn't hear what it was, but Milly let go of his hand and grabbed his arm as if she intended to stop him going after Cash.

Cash put up his fists. *Let's see you try it, buddy! Come on.*

"Stop it!" Milly hissed, her cheeks aflame.

"You stop it," Cash said, looking right at her. "Stop the wedding. Now."

There was dead silence in the church. You could have heard a snowflake fall. Mike's fists were still clenched. Milly's knuckles were white on his arm. Cash rocked on the toes of his boots, eyes narrow, daring him.

At last the minister cleared his throat. "I don't think—" he began tentatively.

Cash didn't think, either, but that wasn't going to stop him. Maybe he'd got here a little later than he would have liked—but he didn't cause the snowstorm, damn it. He'd come to prevent a disaster, and by God, he was going to prevent it.

He turned to face the assembled wedding guests. "When a girl gets married these days, we figure she loves the fella she's marryin'. We reckon she knows her own mind, and that there's only one man in the world for her. Agreed?"

He heard some murmurs of assent, saw some nods.

He nodded, too. "That's what you'd think, all right. But in this case, that's not true."

He heard a sharp gasp behind him. Milly. He glanced back at her. She was glaring at him.

He gave her a faint smile. "I think she likes this fella a whole lot," he allowed, tipping his head in Mike's direction. "She says he's stable. Dependable. She says he's real reliable—" he tried his best to sound admiring of all Mike Dutton's finer traits "—and I believe her. He'd prob'ly make some woman a damn—er, sorry—darn—" he shot a quick glance at the minister who was watching the entire proceedings with morbid fascination "—good husband. But not Milly."

He heard her suck in her breath again, but he didn't look at her this time. He turned and looked at the congregation, searching their faces one by one.

"The guy who marries Milly ought to be more than stable and dependable and reliable," he went on. "He ought to love Milly more than any other guy loves her. And *nobody* loves Milly the way I do." He paused and turned, and now he looked straight at her. "And Milly loves me, too." Another pause. "Don't you?"

He didn't give her a chance to answer. He turned back to the congregation and said, "Tell you what, I'll step back...I'll walk right straight out of here this very minute and let you get on with it—if Milly will swear right here in front of God and all of you that what I've just said isn't true."

He stopped and waited. Months. Weeks. Days. Hours at least. Probably not even a minute. But it seemed like forever to him.

The silence was thunderous.

He'd prayed it would be. Had prayed that Milly wouldn't be able to lie, had trusted that she wouldn't.

There was no sound. No sound at all. The silence went on and on.

He breathed again. Lightly. Shallowly. And then there was the smallest ragged sob.

Oh, cripes. His head jerked around. She was *crying!*

Don't! he wanted to implore her. *Don't cry, for heaven's sake! For* my *sake!*

And then he heard more sniffling, and he looked the other way, and damned if her mother wasn't crying, too! Carole mopped her eyes with a handkerchief and shook her head as she clung to Milly's dad.

Milly's dad looked disgusted. "Oh, for God's sake," he muttered. "I don't believe this."

The minister didn't seem to, either. He cleared his throat, began to speak, then stopped and shook his head. "I've never..." he mumbled, but the words died out.

The only one who seemed to have any presence of mind was good old reliable Dutton. He looked at Cash for a long moment, dark eyes searching. Cash met his gaze determinedly, defiantly. And then finally Dutton turned to Milly. "You want him?" he asked her.

She was still crying. Her face, first pale, then red, was now blotchy. She didn't answer. She gulped and cried harder. Apparently for Dutton that was answer enough.

"Fine," he said. "You got 'im. I'd rather know now." And then he turned and walked out.

No one else moved. They all, except Milly, looked at Cash.

For the first time he was at a loss.

He hadn't thought beyond stopping the wedding. Well, he'd stopped it. Now what?

He looked around—at Milly who, despite her blotchy face and runny eyeliner, was a beautiful bride. He looked at Dori in her bridesmaid dress, shaking her head in astonishment, at a dazed best man he didn't know, but who at least hadn't followed Dutton out the door. He looked at the couple of hundred people who'd braved a winter storm to watch Milly get married.

No reason to send them home as long as there was another willing groom, he decided.

He grinned, relieved, almost cheerful now that he had a grip again. He turned to Milly. "You want to get married? Suits me. Let's get married." He held out a hand to her and stepped forward.

Straight into the bride's right hook.

There was just no pleasing some women.

She'd wanted to marry him, hadn't she? She'd wanted forever. Wasn't that what she'd said?

She'd wanted him to give up riding Deliverance, stick around and convince her. Well, he had. Mostly. He'd given up the horse, given up the rodeo, given up everything. He'd driven through the damnedest storm he'd ever seen to get back to her.

And she not only wouldn't marry him—letting a perfectly good church, a couple hundred guests and a real nice wedding cake go to waste—she wouldn't even listen to him!

She socked him in the jaw and took off.

"What the hell's wrong with her now?" he asked his buddies.

They didn't know. Women were a mystery to them, too, they said. They were all sympathetic, especially Shane.

Shane went way out of his way to tell Cash that he'd done the right thing, that Milly was making a big mistake, that they'd work it all out. He said all the things Cash wanted to hear. He said them a lot—almost as if he was trying to convince himself, not Cash.

Heck, you'd have thought Shane had been the one two-timing him with Milly! But Cash knew better than that.

And he didn't waste much time thinking about Shane. Shane didn't matter.

Nothing mattered—but Milly.

She was the reason, damn it all, that he'd come back.

He'd driven all those miles staring not at the road but at a future without Milly—and finally, *finally,* his head had come to terms with what his heart seemed to have known all along: that what mattered most wasn't Deliverance or winning money or gold buckles or having his freedom or anything else.

What mattered was Milly.

When he had to face the rest of his life knowing that she wouldn't be there for him—that he could never just call and talk to her, or drop in and tease her, or go horseback riding or canoeing with her, or *make love with her*—well, that mattered a whole hell of a lot.

Cash had never given much thought to settling down. It had always seemed like something old folks did. Now he thought it might be something that people who loved each other did—because they wanted to be together, because they wanted to know they could count on each other.

He finally discovered something that scared him more than marriage—the realization that Milly was getting married and that the guy marrying her wasn't going to be him.

Facing a future without Milly was suddenly a whole lot scarier than walking down the aisle and saying, "I do."

He needed Milly. He'd come to count on her in ways that he didn't even yet completely understand, though they'd never really talked about what they meant to each other. Or *he* hadn't, anyway.

He was a guy, for crying out loud. He didn't say mushy things. He didn't even *think* mushy things.

But on the road north in that storm, he'd thought pretty desperate things—like what would happen if he got there too late!

But he hadn't got there too late.

He'd stopped the wedding.

Milly was still free. And someday, she would be his—if he could ever convince her.

Eleven

She wouldn't talk to him. She wouldn't listen to him. She wouldn't even *see* him.

If he walked into her parents' house, she walked out. If he came to Poppy's florist shop, she left. If he showed up at her apartment, she wouldn't answer the door. He tried ordering flowers sent to the motel room where he was staying so she'd have to deliver them; she threw the bouquet in his face. When he tried it again, Poppy delivered them.

"What the hell am I going to do with these?" he demanded, when she shoved a dozen red roses in his face.

"Make potpourri," she suggested. Poppy was no help. She was vague and absentminded and dithery. Not at all the Poppy he was used to.

He tried to talk to Milly's parents, to get them to make her realize how much he cared. They at least listened to him, especially once he offered to help pay the bills from the wedding he'd spoiled.

Her father went so far as to say, "I gotta admit, I admire your guts, boy."

But even he couldn't make Milly see Cash.

"She's a force," he said again.

Yeah, Cash was beginning to figure that out for himself.

Milly's mother was sympathetic. She scolded him for making Milly cry. But then she gave him cups of coffee and patted his arm while he tried to articulate his feelings. But she couldn't make Milly listen, either.

"Our Milly's a little stubborn," she said in what had to be the understatement of the year. "And you did embarrass her."

Like he hadn't embarrassed himself? But, hell, Cash thought, what was a little embarrassment in the larger course of events.

"Too much," Dori informed him. "She would like to kill you."

"Tell her she can," Cash said, desperate. "Tell her I'll wait for her down by the river tonight. Her choice of weapon."

Dori smiled. "That sounds promising."

"Swear you'll tell her."

Dori swore. But Milly never came.

He was at his wit's end.

"What'm I gonna do?" he asked Shane.

"Hang yourself," Shane said. He looked pretty glum these days, too.

"Come for dinner tomorrow night," her mother invited him after two weeks of fruitless attempts to make Milly see reason. "Someone else might be here, too," she added with a smile.

Hoping against hope, Cash came. He was sitting at the kitchen table talking to her mother when "someone else" came in the door.

When Milly saw him, she stopped dead.

"How could you?" she railed at her mother. "You're sleeping with the enemy!"

Cash bolted to his feet so fast he knocked the chair over. "I am *not* sleepin' with your mother!"

Milly didn't answer. She just turned and ran.

Carole put her hand on his arm to stop him going after her. "Figure of speech, my dear."

She couldn't take much more of this.

Everywhere she went in Livingston, people looked at her and whispered. And Milly knew what they were whispering.

Look, there's the girl whose wedding got crashed! What could she have been thinking marrying a man she didn't love? Had she made up with the one who made a fool of her? What had a smart fellow like Mike Dutton seen in a weak-minded idiot like Milly Malone, anyway?

Milly wondered the same things herself—about everything except whether or not she and Cash had made up.

They hadn't. They weren't going to. *Ever.*

She was adamant about that. She told her mother, her father, Dori, Poppy, everyone who would listen.

She didn't tell Cash.

She wouldn't talk to him. She was sure she wouldn't need to.

He might hang around a day or two—"until Tuesday," she would mutter bitterly every time she thought about it— but before long, she knew there would be a horse to ride somewhere down the road, and he would be off again, chasing that gold buckle and his freedom.

It wasn't that he always left—that there was always another horse, another rodeo or another gold buckle—that bothered Milly. It was that somehow, wanting those things meant to him that he couldn't also want her.

With Cash it had always been one or the other. Never both.

Milly didn't understand. She never would.

But it didn't matter now. It was good, in fact. It meant that he would be gone soon. And when he was, she would pick up the pieces and get on with her life.

The trouble was, he didn't go.

Instead of heading off to points south and gold buckles galore, he got a job working for Noah Tanner and Taggart Jones. They taught bronc-and-bull-riding to hopeful rodeo cowboys on Taggart's ranch up near Elmer. Cash, Poppy told her, was helping out with their schools.

"Here?" Milly was aghast. "He's staying here?"

"In Elmer. That's what I heard, anyway," Poppy said vaguely. She didn't say who she'd heard it from.

"He won't stay," Milly said. She hoped.

But the fates conspired against her. Next thing she knew he was also working for Jed McCall.

"Jed broke his arm," Poppy said. "He needs someone to feed cattle and help with the calving."

"Field work?" Milly said, disbelieving.

Cash would never do field work, Milly was certain. But the next time she saw him he was buying a tractor part. She turned on her heel and rapidly walked the other way.

It didn't matter that he was hanging around, she told herself. Out at Jones's ranch or up at Jed McCall's, he might as well be in San Antonio or Phoenix. She never went there. She wouldn't have to see him.

Three days later she stopped at the grocery store, and damned if Cash wasn't unloading boxes there!

"What are you doing here?" Milly demanded shrilly. She looked from him to her father accusingly.

Her father gave a vague, helpless shrug and said, "He offered to help."

Cash gave her a hard smile. "I'm settlin' in."

She didn't believe it. *Wouldn't* believe it.

She tried not to think about him. But he was like that credit card in the commercial on TV—everywhere she wanted to be! She felt some nights that if she rolled over in bed, Cash would be there beside her.

In the flesh, he wasn't.

In her mind, heaven help her, he was.

Spring was upon them in earnest. The leaves were coming out on the trees. The sheep had baby lambs frolicking after them. The mamma cows were calving. Still Cash didn't go away.

Milly knew then that she'd have to.

Livingston—not just Livingston—*Montana* wasn't big enough for both of them!

Milly made up her mind to leave. She needed space. Distance. A new life. She'd been going to have one once before, hadn't she? She'd been going to go to Denver.

What was to stop her going now?

Her father was doing fine. Now that Jake was in school all day, Dori was almost an equal partner. They had a new stock boy helping out. They even had Cash, for goodness' sake!

If he wanted to stay here, let him.

She would be the one to leave this time.

"She's what?" Cash didn't believe his ears. He stared at Milly's mother, who kept right on stirring the pot on the stove.

She spared him a sympathetic glance. "Moving to Denver. She told us last night."

"Got a chance to buy into a business," Milly's dad added. "She says it's a great opportunity." He sounded hearty, but Cash knew him well enough now to hear the false bravado in his words. He didn't sound any more convinced than Cash felt, and he was looking at Cash as if Milly's decision to leave was all his fault.

Well, according to Milly, he was sure it was.

He'd had plenty of time to realize how humiliated she'd been at the wedding where she didn't marry Dutton. He'd heard enough from Shane and Jed and Taggart and Mace Nichols and their wives to know that they were the talk of the valley.

"You're more famous than those Hollywood fellas," Jed had told him just last week.

"Still?"

Jed nodded. "Reckon you'll be the talk of the town till Redford does another movie hereabouts."

"Swell." *Hurry up, Redford!* "What can I do?" Cash asked.

"Marry her," Jed suggested. "That'd put an end to it."

"What the hell do you think I'm tryin' to do?" Cash almost exploded.

"She still won't listen? It's been months. How long you gonna wait?"

"Forever," Cash said. He meant it, too.

He'd show her that he knew life was no eight-second ride—if it took him eighty years!

It was hard because every day he saw things he wanted to tell her about, to share with her and watch her smile. There were baby lambs on the hillsides now. Some of the more innovative ranchers were running both sheep and cattle. Some had baby buffalo here and there, too. There was nothing funnier than a just-born baby buffalo wobbling after its mom. Even calves, too, were pretty amazing.

He'd done a lot of rodeoing, but he'd never stayed in one place long enough to do much real cowboy work. He found he liked it. The world didn't go by in such a whirl as it did when he was going down the road. He had time to stop and appreciate the little things, the subtle things.

And all time to miss Milly that there was in the world.

Brenna, Jed's wife, had a baby while Cash was working for them. He'd never paid much attention to babies before. He couldn't ever remember being impressed by one. But, like the lambs and the calves and the buffalo, little Shannon McCall was pretty amazing.

He remembered Milly talking about "their kids." Then the words had sent a shaft of panic straight through him. Now it didn't seem like such a bad idea at all. He wanted to tell her, to talk to her about it.

Except Milly still wasn't talking—or listening—to him. She was moving to Denver instead.

It was too much to hope that Cash wouldn't come to Poppy Hamilton's wedding. It was, after all, Cash's rodeo buddy, Shane Nichols, that Poppy was marrying.

Milly couldn't believe it when Poppy told her. *"Shane?"* she'd said when Poppy told her that morning in the florist's shop. "You don't even know him!"

Poppy had turned as red as her name and cleared her throat and looked out the window at something that must have been really interesting. Then she shrugged sort of awkwardly and said, "Well, I do now."

"Obviously," Milly replied drily, then looked at Poppy intently. "How did you meet? It wasn't Cash who introduced you, was it?"

"Of course not," Poppy said hotly, her color still abnormally high. "The whole world doesn't revolve around you, you know!"

Milly felt her own cheeks burn. "I know that. I just...thought... Never mind." She went back to work on the flowers she was arranging.

Poppy gave her arm a pat. "I didn't mean to jump on you. It's just...you've got to get over this. You've got to move on."

"I *am* moving on," Milly reminded her. "I'm going to Denver at the end of the month, remember?"

"That's not moving on," Poppy said flatly. "That's running away."

Milly's head jerked up. "You're on *his* side?"

"I'm not on anyone's side," Poppy said patiently "I just hate to see two people who love each other—"

"I do not love Cash!"

Poppy just looked at her.

It seemed to Milly that everyone at Poppy and Shane's wedding was looking at her now. She was still a local curiosity—the girl who didn't know her own mind.

She felt as if all eyes were on her wherever she went. Well, maybe not *all* eyes. Some people were watching Mike. And some were watching Cash. Wondering if they were going to come to blows, perhaps?

Milly tried very hard not to look at either one of them.

She was quite sure Mike didn't want to see her. And God knew she didn't want to see Cash!

That was why she stayed aware of every move Cash made. Because she wanted to avoid him, *not* because she cared!

It didn't matter to her if he talked to every pretty female under the age of forty in the room. She didn't care if he danced with them, either.

But somehow it was easier to breathe when he was talking to Poppy's father, the judge, or to Shane's brother, Mace, or to Taggart and Felicity Jones or Noah and Tess Tanner or Jed and Brenna McCall.

He seemed to have developed a circle of friends in the valley. He even spent some time chatting with Rance Phillips, the guy Poppy's father had wanted her to marry.

Why couldn't Cash have behaved like Rance? Milly wondered irritably. Rance hadn't broken up Shane and

Poppy's wedding, even though he was Poppy's father's choice for a groom. No, he came with a date, danced with the bride and behaved like a sane adult.

Not like some men she could mention.

If Cash had behaved like that, she'd be Mrs. Mike Dutton now.

She glanced in Mike's direction. He was standing by the bar talking to Lisa, the girl who worked in the outfitter's shop below Milly's apartment. They were laughing and, as Milly watched, Mike put his hand on Lisa's arm and said something right into her ear.

Milly felt nothing. No jealousy. No envy. No wish that it was her arm he was touching. She actually felt glad, relieved. At least Mike's life hadn't been destroyed by her idiocy. He was moving on.

Just like her.

As if he sensed her thoughts, Mike looked around just then and saw her looking at him. Immediately Milly looked away. But not before she saw Mike say something to Lisa, then move purposefully toward her.

Please, no! Milly cast around for a quick escape. But there was none—except the door behind where Cash stood talking to Shane's brother. She turned, desperate, and spotted Jake, his nose pressed against the window glass, obviously far more interested in whatever was outside than the wedding reception in here. She'd go get him and take him out for a while. Poor little kid had to be bored stiff.

But before she could, Mike was there. "Still haven't made up?"

"What?" Milly blinked, then began edging away. But he caught her fingers and anchored her where she stood. He leaned against the wall next to her, so that they stood together ostensibly watching the other couples dance.

But Milly knew Mike's eyes were on Cash. And even

though Cash kept on talking to Mace, Milly could feel Cash's eyes on her.

"You know what I mean," Mike said easily.

She would have liked to have pretended she didn't, but she'd already made enough of a fool of herself where Mike was concerned. There was nothing to be gained by pretending.

"No, we haven't," she said, refusing to look at either one of them. "And we never will."

"Never is a long time," Mike said mildly, still staring across the room. Then he looked down at Milly and added quietly, "Almost as long as forever." Then he took her hand. "Dance with me."

"You don't want to—"

"I wanted to marry you," Mike said firmly, pulling her gently but inexorably into his arms. "I think I can be trusted to decide whether or not I want to dance with you." His eyes met hers. "Come on, Milly. Dance."

They danced. It was a slow dance. An easy-listening, easy-dancing number—soft swaying music that seeped into a person's soul and set it free. And, moving to the music, Milly began to breathe more easily for the first time that day. Something tight inside her began to loosen. She felt the tension in her—the tension that had been in her so long she couldn't even remember a time it hadn't been there— begin to relax, to release.

She knew what he was doing. He was forgiving her. He was saying he understood. He accepted. He was here, dancing with her, to tell her that.

He was setting things right between them—and making sure everyone knew it.

Milly blinked back a tear, then smiled up at him. "Thank you," she whispered.

Mike smiled at her. "My pleasure." And then he danced

her across the floor, and his arms loosened, and he stepped back and turned her—

Into Cash's arms.

Cash appeared as startled as she was. And as desperate, she noted, as he looked in astonishment from her to Mike.

Milly shook her head and started to back away. *What on earth do you think you're doing?* she asked Mike silently.

He smiled encouragement at her. "He said he loves you," Mike reminded her. "From what I've seen the past couple of months, he's been trying to show you he loves you." Then he looked at Cash. "Maybe you'd better tell her again."

And then, in the silence—and it *was* silent, because virtually everyone in the hall had stopped dead at the sight of Mike turning Milly into Cash's arms—he did.

He looked straight into her eyes and said, "I love you." His voice was low and ragged, and this time Milly didn't think anyone heard him but her.

"Don't leave," he said equally quietly. "Please don't leave." He swallowed, and she saw the pain in his eyes. "Or take me with you if you do."

Milly blinked. She didn't speak. Her thoughts, which had been in a whirl so long she'd grown accustomed to it, suddenly seemed to stop. Her anger—the anger she'd lived on—stilled. It was as if a great crashing storm had abated, as if the noise and clamor had ceased, as if the clouds had lifted and rolled away—and left her there looking clearly for the first time at the man who had been the reason for it all.

He looked back, not speaking—just looking—his heart in his eyes.

Cash. Whom she loved.

Who loved her.

She knew that now. Perhaps she'd always known it. He wouldn't have come back if he hadn't.

She'd accused him of crashing the wedding to embarrass her, of pulling his grandstanding trick to win himself some more time to play before he ever—*if* he ever—got serious.

But it wasn't true.

She knew it hadn't been true. Not since he'd turned around wherever it was he'd turned around—and come back to her. *Then.* Not on Tuesday.

He had learned. And he was here for the long haul, not for eight seconds. He'd come to stay. He'd proved that.

But she hadn't been willing to admit it.

Because, she admitted to herself now, she was scared, too.

It was easier to blame him than to admit that she was scared she wouldn't be enough for him, that he'd get bored with her, that someday he'd leave her because she wasn't enough of a woman to hang on to a man like him.

It seemed safer not to let him in than someday to be the one left.

Was she going to go through life playing it safe forever?

Forever, as Mike pointed out, was a very long time. A long time to do without love. A long time to live without Cash.

She didn't want to live without Cash.

She wanted to live with him—to share the risks of life with him. It wouldn't even be living if she had to be without him. All the anger, all the fury, had been a cover—a protection.

She felt as if they'd both been stripped bare—all their needs, all their hopes, all their inadequacies visible to each other.

It was scary, yes. But it was good. It wasn't pretence; it was real.

"I love you," she whispered, and tears started to run down her face. "Oh, Cash, I love you, too."

* * *

He *hated* it when women cried.

One woman, anyway. Because of him. Because she loved him.

It didn't make sense. Why on earth would you cry because you loved someone, unless you thought he was going to leave you, which Cash absolutely and definitely was never ever going to do?

He was Milly's—heart and soul, mind and body, for ever and ever—if only she'd quit!

"Aw, hell, Milly, don't!" he begged, gripping her hands. "Don't cry. I don't know what to do when you cry!"

"Hold me," she muttered against his shirtfront. "Just hold me."

So he did. He wrapped his arms around her and pulled her hard against him. He pressed his face into her hair and breathed deep. A shudder ran through him, a shudder of need, of longing, of promise unfulfilled. It had been so long, so very long.

"Love me," she whispered.

He jumped. "Here?" he exclaimed, aghast, looking around at the crowd of a couple of hundred interested wedding guests.

Milly giggled. She pulled back and looked into his eyes. "Kiss me here," she said. "Love me at home." She tipped her face up to his. "For the rest of our lives."

"Oh, yes," he promised. And then he slipped his arms around her again and touched his lips to hers—at first gently, then deeply, then soul shatteringly.

Somewhere in another galaxy he heard applause and laughter and kids whooping and hollering.

When at last he stepped back, Mike gave him a thumbs-up sign, Dori gave them a nod of satisfaction, Jake looked at his mother and beamed. Milly's parents looked at each other, then at Cash and Milly, and breathed a sigh of relief.

The minister blinked, then smiled bemusedly, looking as if he'd been there, done that—and expected that he was going to have to do it again sometime very soon.

Cash pretty much thought he was dreaming.

A part of him fully expected to wake up in the middle of the night and discover that he was alone.

But when he awoke, it was with Milly in his arms. It was with Milly's arms around him. He sighed. He stretched a little, then eased himself back to look at her in the moonlight that spilled through the window, to convince himself that this—that *she*—was real.

As he did so, she stirred and slowly opened her eyes. She smiled at him.

It was the smile he had been afraid he would never see again. It was the most precious, the most beautiful smile on earth. He smiled, too, then felt something damp at the corner of his eye.

Oh hell, he wasn't going to cry, too, was he?

And then he thought, so what if he did? It didn't matter. What mattered was Milly. Loving Milly.

It had taken him long enough to realize it. He wasn't going to forget it in a hurry. There would, he hoped, be lots of laughter and maybe a few tears for them over the years. But whatever there was, they would share it—together. Here. Denver. Wherever life took them.

None of it mattered but that they were together.

Milly eased herself up and kissed the corner of his eye. She tasted the tear and then she kissed him again with all her heart. "Ah, Cash. I love you," she said against his lips.

"I love you, too," he told her, his voice rough with emotion.

And he always would.

* * * * *

THE TALLCHIEFS

the beloved miniseries by
USA Today bestselling author

Cait London

continues with
RAFE PALLADIN:
MAN OF SECRETS

(SD #1160)

Available August 1998

When takeover tycoon Rafe Palladin set out to *acquire* Demi Tallchief as part of a business deal, Demi had a few conditions of her own. And Rafe had some startling secrets to reveal....

    "Cait London is one of the best writers in contemporary romance today."   —*Affaire de Coeur*

And coming from Desire in **December 1998,** look for **The Perfect Fit** in which *Man of the Month* Nick Palladin lures Ivory Tallchief back home to Amen Flats, Wyoming.

Available at your favorite retail outlet.

MATERNITY LEAVE

Coming September 1998

Three delightful stories about the blessings
and surprises of "Labor" Day.

TABLOID BABY by Candace Camp

She was whisked to the hospital in the nick of time....

THE NINE-MONTH KNIGHT
by Cait London

A down-on-her-luck secretary is experiencing
odd little midnight cravings....

THE PATERNITY TEST by Sherryl Woods

The stick turned blue before her
biological clock struck twelve....

*These three special women are very pregnant...and very
single, although they won't be either for too much longer,
because baby—and Daddy—are on their way!*

Available at your favorite retail outlet.

HERE COME THE
Virgin Brides!

Celebrate the joys of first love with **more unforgettable stories from Romance's brightest stars:**

SWEET BRIDE OF REVENGE
by Suzanne Carey—June 1998 (SR #1300)

Reader favorite Suzanne Carey weaves a sensuously powerful tale about a man who forces the daughter of his enemy to be his bride of revenge. But what happens when this hard-hearted husband falls head over heels…for his wife?

THE BOUNTY HUNTER'S BRIDE
by Sandra Steffen—July 1998 (SR #1306)

In this provocative page-turner by beloved author Sandra Steffen, a shotgun wedding is only the beginning when an injured bounty hunter and the sweet seductress who'd nursed him to health are discovered in a remote mountain cabin by her gun-toting dad and *four* brothers!

SUDDENLY…MARRIAGE!
by Marie Ferrarella—August 1998 (SR #1312)

RITA Award-winning author Marie Ferrarella weaves a magical story set in sultry New Orleans about two people determined to remain single who exchange vows in a mock ceremony during Mardi Gras, only to learn their bogus marriage is the real thing.…

And look for more VIRGIN BRIDES in future months,
only in—

▼ *Silhouette* ROMANCE™

Available at your favorite retail outlet.

Look us up on-line at: http://www.romance.net

SRVBJ-A

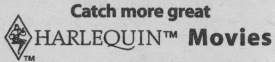